Look for the following ebook prequels to
The Eye of Odin

Double Cross
An Eye of Odin Short Prequel #1

Fated
An Eye of Odin Short Prequel #2

THE RAIDERS OF FOLKLORE

THE EYE OF ODIN

DENNIS STAGINNUS

STAG'S HEAD BOOKS

The Eye of Odin
The Raiders of Folklore – Book 1
Copyright © 2015 Stag's Head Books

Published by Stag's Head Books

Cover Design: Pintado
Illustrations: Jennifer Pendergast
Book Design: Maureen Cutajar

Visit the author's website at:
www.dennisstaginnus.com

ISBN 978-0-9936824-4-5

For Shannon
The source of magic in my life

Prologue

April, 2003
Baghdad, Iraq

I n the moments before her death, Rachel Finn breathed in the earthy smell of dust and broken brick. Thunderclaps echoed overhead, the low drumming bass of artillery shells raining down on the Iraqi capital. The walls and ceiling shuddered. Looters rushed through the corridors above, scavenging the remains of the National Museum like vultures picking away at a carcass. The war provided the perfect cover, the perfect distraction to steal what Rachel had come for—the fragment of a Viking runestone hidden and all but forgotten in the museum's basement vaults.

She never suspected her killers had followed her into the labyrinth of catacombs twisting beneath the building's foundations. It wasn't until a shadow emerged behind her, eclipsing the vault's flickering lights, that she realized she wasn't alone. Rarely had anyone crept up on her so easily.

Rachel turned. The silhouette of a man stood a few feet away. She noticed too late the polished muzzle of a pistol in his hand. The weapon fired twice. The first bullet grazed her side, but the second tore into her chest, puncturing a lung.

She slumped against the stone wall, blood seeping between her fingers.

A second man, with slicked-back hair and a neatly trimmed goatee, stepped forward. He wore sunglasses despite the dim lighting. "Give me that, you idiot," he said, grabbing the gun from the shooter's hand. "You could've hit the stone."

He ignored Rachel's bleeding body, walking past her without a second glance, and knelt in front of the artifact. He studied the inscriptions carved onto its dark surface.

The faint hint of a smile creased his lips. "This is it—one of the pieces of Mimir's Stone."

"The bottom piece, by the looks of it," the shooter noted.

Rachel swallowed. "Do not go searching for it," she croaked, guessing the man's intentions. Why else would he have been down here when more valuable relics waited upstairs? "You don't know the consequences of what you might unleash."

By itself, the fragment—and the inscriptions it held—were meaningless. But together, combined with the other four pieces, it would describe the location of an artifact few people knew existed.

The man turned and crouched next to her. "I know exactly what I'm doing, witch," he said, caressing her hair with the back of his fingers.

Rachel could see the reflection of her crumpled figure in his lenses. She opened her mouth to plead with him, but convulsed in painful spasms.

The man stood. "You are lucky to die so quickly," he said. "I will be less merciful to your kind once I have the artifact."

Then he and the shooter hefted the stone from its resting place and exited the vault. The sounds of their shuffling feet faded down the maze of corridors.

Rachel tried to drag herself after them, leaving crimson smears on the concrete floor. No use—her legs refused to cooperate.

She propped herself against the wall, struggling to keep her eyes open. She turned and faced the black emptiness where the runestone had sat for centuries. Blinking away tears, she thought of her daughter. She would grow up without a mother, in a world where an ancient artifact could bring about mankind's destruction.

Her breath hitched. Another painful spasm wracked her body. Blood bubbled from her lips. The edges of her vision clouded and the thud of her heartbeat slowed. She felt the tightness in her lungs as the life drained from her body. The runestone's inscriptions haunted her final conscious thought:

"From shadows blind to greed and sin,
Beware the Eye of Odin."

Chapter 1

Years later.
Vancouver, Canada

Sylvester Zito angled his rusted brown Chevy toward the Vancouver Museum. From his mouth dangled a cigarette. A long ash quivered, threatening to break free at any moment.

"Don't screw this up," he warned, focusing on the road. "You know what's at stake."

Grayle Rowen tightened the grip on his backpack. The fifteen-year-old knew exactly what was at stake: enough money to last a lifetime. Zito wouldn't say how much, but the greedy look in his eyes and the spittle building on his lips indicated it must have been a fair sum.

"Did you hear me? Don't mess this up."

"I heard you," Grayle said through clenched teeth.

The Chevy screeched to a halt. Zito grabbed him roughly by the shoulder. The jagged scar on the man's hand pointed at Grayle like a fleshy lightning bolt. "Don't take that tone with me," he said, the cigarette bouncing between his lips. "This could be my big break, and you're not gonna wreck it. You got me?"

Grayle tugged free of his grasp and opened the car door.

"Here." Zito held out a smartphone.

"But I'm not—"

"Just take it," Zito snarled. "How else am I gonna keep tabs on you?"

Grayle was banned from owning digital devices of any kind, a condition of his parole. He took the phone and stuffed it in his pocket. This job was worth a little parole violation.

"I'll be around the corner, so don't get any bright ideas," Zito added, waiting for him to get out. "And don't screw this—"

Grayle slammed the door before Zito could finish. He flung his backpack over his shoulder and trudged toward the museum's entrance.

Gears ground and tires squealed as the Chevy sped off behind him.

Grayle turned, watching it disappear around a corner in a cloud of black exhaust. *That's it. This is the last job I do for them.* For seven months he'd had to put up with Zito and his wife, his current foster parents. In that time, he'd stolen for them several times, jeopardizing his freedom and the new life he had. For the first time ever, he was in a regular school, leading a normal life—as normal a life as he could remember, anyway. Five years earlier, he'd been found wandering the woods in Stanley Park, cold and alone. Everything before that point was a fog that refused to lift. So, in all honesty, no matter what Zito thought, Grayle didn't want to screw this up.

Honestly, my life is screwed up enough as it is.

Four school buses pulled into the unloading zone ahead, carrying the rest of his ninth-grade class. Grayle wasn't allowed to ride with them—something about preventing him from "influencing the upstanding students of Bayview Secondary School." He didn't mind. Everybody avoided him anyway—just the way he liked it.

Students spilled onto the sidewalk. Most gave him a wide berth while others did their best to ignore him. He'd grown used to being an outcast, hearing the whispers behind his back:

"He doesn't know where he came from."

"Don't stand too close—he'll pick your pocket."

"He's been to juvie."

"I heard he burned down his last foster home."

"This guy, he told a friend of my cousin's boyfriend that he robbed a bank."

Stuff like that.

The problem was the rumors were all true—maybe not exactly as they told it but accurate for the most part.

Britney Astor brushed by, clutching a red Coach bag closer to her body. Her friend, Carrigan Murphy, did the same.

Grayle acknowledged them with a crooked grin.

He'd broken into the Astor family mansion a few weeks ago, stealing cash and jewellery. The break-in had prompted Britney's father to beef up their home security. Nothing Grayle couldn't handle. To prove it, he broke in again a week later, stealing Britney's housecat, Puddles. He'd grown fond of the animal, keeping it for a few days before returning it. Grayle remembered the look on Britney's face when Puddles mysteriously reappeared in her homeroom at school.

"Keep moving, Rowen," muttered Mr. Snodgrass, peering down his long, thin nose at Grayle. The substitute history teacher's resemblance to a vulture was uncanny. "No funny business today. It would be a shame to suspend you from yet another school."

"Yes, sir," Grayle answered with an exaggerated military salute.

He followed his class up the museum's marble steps and through four columns framing the entrance like an ancient Greek temple. Bright red banners hung from each stone pillar, providing a splash of color to the building's otherwise drab façade. Barricades had been erected on either side of the entrance to keep crowds from storming the building.

Hardly the place any typical teenager would be fighting to get into, Grayle thought. *Unless you're a history nerd, or something special was happening inside.*

Three twelve-years-old girls stood next to the barricade off to his right, shaking with nervous anticipation. They held a sign that read: "We're you're #1 fans, Jameson."

"Jameson" being Jameson Blaze, the famous pop star scheduled to perform at the museum's grand re-opening and the only reason the field trip was so well attended on a Friday afternoon.

The classes were ushered through the entryway along a red, velvet-roped maze leading into the building's newly renovated rotunda. Natural light flooded from a glass dome high above.

Grayle scanned the ceiling and doorways, spotting security cameras and motion sensors. He'd been trained to hone his criminal senses, learning to analyze a room's security measures in a matter of seconds.

The click-clacking of heels on marble redirected his attention.

A woman in a blue skirt and matching suit jacket made her way to a makeshift stage erected at the far end of the rotunda. Her hair was wrapped in a tight bun, and her horn-rimmed glasses seemed too large for her angular face. A dozen similarly dressed guides followed on her heels. The woman stepped on the stage. A "Mysteries of the Vikings" banner hung from a backdrop behind her. She settled behind a lectern and tapped a microphone, making sure it was on.

"Good morning."

Except for the A students, everyone else paid her no attention.

"Good morning!" she repeated more harshly. Feedback from the speakers squealed across the room.

The group fell silent.

"Welcome to the Vancouver Museum. I'm Miss Jennings. We are thrilled to have young guests attending our grand reopening"—she sounded more irritated than thrilled—"but our staff must ask you to respect the following rules."

The classes let out a collective groan.

"First, keep your hands off the glass casings protecting the artifacts. Second, no food is permitted in the exhibits—"

Austin Moxey popped his bubble gum, causing a wave of rebellious snickers.

Jennings scowled, easily picking out the gangly boy in his yellow shirt and spiked hair. "Third, no running is allowed anywhere on the premises. Fourth…"

Grayle tuned out the woman's list of *no*s and *don't*s. He saw Britney on her phone, texting as usual. Fletcher Thomas stood beside her, pulling a finger from his ear and inspecting what he'd found.

Nice.

Some believed too many blows to Fletcher's head playing hockey had left him incapable of higher brain function. Most admitted he'd always been that way.

Britney made a face and turned her back to him.

Carrigan twirled a finger in her hair, talking up Alistair Thorn. She batted her eyelashes and swayed her hips. He didn't seem interested in what she had to say, focused instead on someone else in the crowd. Grayle followed his line of vision. He glimpsed Sarah Finn staring—but not at Alistair. She was staring at *him*.

Grayle turned away, not sure whether it was the "good" kind of staring or the "you're a leper" kind. More than once, he'd felt her drowning gaze. Her bright blue eyes were hard to ignore, and so was her coolness, her smile, and her raven black hair that cascaded down well past her shoulders.

"…rules exist in order to preserve the museum's collection," Jennings continued. "Please respect all areas with heightened security." She paused, running her eyes over the audience as if committing their faces to memory. "You'll be finishing your tour at the 'Mysteries of the Vikings' grand opening. Celebrities will be present for the ribbon cutting ceremony, so—"

"We love Jameson!" chorused a group of girls.

Jennings frowned at the outburst. "So you are expected to be on your best behavior. Until the ceremony begins, enjoy the museum's collections. Please find your teachers, and a tour guide will be assigned to you."

The next hour passed in a blur. Grayle trailed after his assigned group through two thousand years of history, staring at too many Greek vases, too many Egyptian hieroglyphs, and way too many naked statues. Ignoring the ramblings of their tour guide, some pimple-faced college student, his classmates would stop and gawk at something that caught their eye, but for the most part, they giggled their way from room to room.

Grayle eyed the gold-and-jewel-encrusted artifacts in the secured display cases. Just one necklace—one small, golden figurine—would be enough to live on for several months, if not years.

But the terms of this assignment were clear: "Complete this heist, and we'll tell you where you came from." That knowledge was worth more to Grayle than any treasure. For the time being though, he'd have to play out this student-on-a-field-trip charade until he got the signal.

Entering the ancient Rome exhibit, Grayle was drawn to a large glass case labeled Gladiator Weapons. An eight-foot-long trident stretched the length of the cabinet—its three bronze tips gleamed in the low light. He wondered how many gladiators it had killed for the favor of the emperor.

A girl and her mother stood next to him, admiring the Roman craftsmanship. The mother put an arm around her daughter as she pointed to a *gladius*—a gladiator's short sword. Grayle noted their easy affection curiously. He never felt sorry for himself for not having parents. He'd learned to live with the ignorance. Deep inside though, he wondered if they were somewhere out there, looking for their lost son. Delusional, really, but the hope got him through difficult times.

He never noticed Sarah coming up beside him until he caught the scent of her perfume. She bent over, staring at the gladiator weapons in morbid fascination.

"Pretty cool, huh?" she said.

Her proximity made his skin tingle. "I guess," he replied, trying to act casual.

"Did you know each weapon was used by a specific gladiator, to kill an opponent in their own unique way?" She looked up. Her blue eyes washed over him like a waterfall.

"No, I didn't." He turned away, focusing on the gladius again.

"They're also a reminder of what people do to one another," she added.

Grayle nodded. "Don't you mean *did* to one another? Fighting to the death in arenas is a thing of the past."

Sarah looked as though she was about to argue. "You're in Snodgrass's class, right?" she asked instead.

"How'd you guess?"

"Well, you're not in mine, and with the way he keeps looking over here with a not-so-friendly look on his face, I did the math."

Grayle glanced over his shoulder. Snodgrass didn't bother turning away, staring at him like a warden eyes a prisoner. "It's a pleasure being under his watchful eye."

Sarah laughed. "I'm sure."

They moved on together from one Roman artifact to the next. Sarah knew her stuff, just about as much as the tour guide. She spoke of legends he'd never heard before, quoting books from people with weird names like Virgil, Ovid, and Livy.

Grayle forgot about his assignment and lost himself in the way Sarah tucked her loose, black flyaways behind her ears and how her upper lip curled slightly when she talked. A part of him expected some practical joke to play out, that she was spending time with him to win a bet or cause some other kind of trouble. But nothing like that happened. She didn't look over her shoulder to see what her friends were doing or to trade a secretive glance that would tell others, *Look at me… I'm with the convicted thief.* She seemed focused on him and, just for a second, Grayle thought she might genuinely be interested in him.

Great.

Any other time, he would have loved to chat up one of the cutest girls in school, but right now?

Bzzzt.

The smartphone vibrated in his pocket.

"Is that yours?" Sarah asked.

"What?" he said, playing dumb and not doing a very good job at it.

Bzzzt.

"Your phone. It's buzzing in your pocket."

Grayle took it out and turned, hiding the device from Snodgrass's view. "It's my fo-rent," he said, looking at the phone's display.

She cocked an eyebrow. "Fo-rent?"

"Foster parent. Probably wants to make sure I haven't burned down the place."

He scanned Zito's text message: "Object inside Viking exhibit. More instructions to follow. Don't screw this up."

"You know, there are rumors about you burning down houses," Sarah said.

"That's all they are... rumors," he lied, putting the phone back in his pocket.

She didn't look convinced.

He got that look a lot.

Their group emerged at the entrance to the Mysteries of the Vikings exhibit. Grayle glanced at the reinforced locking mechanisms protecting whatever lay inside. By the looks of it, nothing short of a blowtorch or a small amount of C4 could penetrate it. Not that it mattered—he wouldn't be breaking in that way.

The tour guide brought their attention to a display case featuring Viking helmets, one of which still had a human skull tucked inside. "That's how the archaeologists found it," the guide explained. "They believe he may have been decapitated during battle, due to the cut marks found along the base of his neck here," he pointed to the remaining vertebrae clinging to the skull.

Students crowded around to get a better look.

"Where are the horns?" Austin asked. "On the helmet, I mean."

"There's no evidence to suggest Vikings ever had horns on their helmets," the guide said. "Our popular image of a Viking comes from artwork and romanticized operas created during the eighteenth and nineteenth centuries, six hundred years after the Viking Age. But I can tell you one thing"—he paused and pointed to the artifact—"there's nothing romantic about a Viking. This particular helmet is believed to have belonged to a berserker, a ruthless warrior who often ran into battle wearing only a bearskin, or nothing at all, to show his courage."

"Eww!" Carrigan cringed.

"I'd probably start laughing, seeing some naked dude coming at me." Austin snorted, nudging Fletcher with his elbow.

"Maybe so, but you wouldn't be laughing for long," the guide said. "In their enraged state, berserkers went completely mad, covering their bodies with blood, howling like wild animals and biting the edges of their shields. They would cut down—"

"Fifteen-year-old girls?" Austin asked.

"Anyone in their path… friend or foe. If you crossed a berserker during battle, you were as good as dead."

The room fell silent.

Grayle watched Carrigan's face glisten in a clammy sweat. The mere mention of blood or other bodily fluids made her gag.

"Oh c'mon, man, that's so lame." Fletcher said, his voice low and slurred. "I could take a pansy Berserker like that." He faked a turning kick and karate chopped the air.

Giggles trickled through the group.

The tour guide raised an eyebrow. "Really? In the heat of battle, you think you could vanquish a six-foot crazed warrior who's made it his life's ambition to kill whatever stood in his way?"

Fletcher didn't answer, probably trying to figure out what *vanquish* meant.

"What's this?" Grayle asked, pointing to a gruesome hook-like weapon in another display case. He hardly ever spoke in class, so hearing his voice drew everyone's attention.

"That was used while performing the Blood Eagle, a rather grisly form of torture."

"What kind of torture?" Carrigan swallowed, her complexion turning a sickly green.

The guide must have noticed. "I'm afraid it may be too graphic to describe," he said delicately. "Trust me, you don't want to—"

"I know what they did," Sarah said. "The Blood Eagle was performed by cutting the ribs of a victim along the spine. Then they reached inside his torso, separating the ribs in such a way that they came out through his back like window shutters." She made a ripping motion with her hands. "Then they pulled the lungs out, placing them on the victim's shoulders so they looked like blood-stained wings."

Carrigan made a retching sound.

"Can you imagine the amount of blood as your insides are torn open?" Sarah added.

Carrigan gagged, threw her hand over her mouth, and bolted for the nearest washroom.

Britney whipped around, scowling at Sarah. "What is wrong with you?" she said before running after her friend.

Even Austin's jaw hung open. "Dude, that was cold."

The reactions didn't seem to faze Sarah. She shrugged and leaned over to examine the hook-like weapon more closely.

Snodgrass sighed. "Wait here, everyone. I will attend to Miss Murphy. The rest of you stay put." His gaze fell on Grayle, the message no doubt specifically intended for him.

Grayle grinned as the history teacher turned and left. Things couldn't have worked out more perfectly.

One teacher down, one artifact to go.

Chapter 2

Sarah watched Grayle melt into the crowd forming inside the museum's rotunda. No one from their school group seemed to notice—or care—he was gone. She was about to follow when her cell phone rang.

"Are you in the exhibit? Do you have it?" asked Grigsby, her Caretaker.

Sarah's jaw tightened. "No. I haven't had a chance—"

"Yer runnin' outta time," he interrupted. "Quit beatin' the devil around the stump an' get it now."

"I'm doing my best." Sometimes she hated his cowboy slang. "I'm going to get Grayle to help me."

"Pull in yer horns, girl," Grigsby warned, his way of telling her to quit looking for trouble. "You know what he is. He's too unpredictable, an' that makes 'im even more dangerous."

"Too much is at stake. If I don't get it today, we may never get another chance."

"I know," the Caretaker agreed, "an' that's what worries me. This whole situation is too convenient, but gettin' the kid involved may further jeopardize the mission."

Miss Jennings walked by. Her face twisted in disapproval at seeing Sarah on her phone. "I'll get the job done," Sarah said, cupping the device with both hands. "Gotta go."

She returned the phone to her bag and glanced at her watch. 3:30.

Thirty minutes before the Viking exhibit officially opened. Half an hour to steal the runestone and less than that to escape without getting caught.

This isn't going to be easy.

She watched security guards positioning themselves at every entrance and exit, making it all the more clear she needed a thief to get into the exhibit. She needed Grayle.

Pushing her way through the crowd, she searched the rotunda. The people appeared as a jumble of glowing auras to her eyes, blending together like watercolours on a canvas. Sarah could see the spectral light radiating off living things, a skill only a handful of witches possessed.

She lowered her mental barrier. The auras brightened to a harsh shine, and the buzz of their emotions hit her like a slap in the face. Along with seeing people's auras came the unfortunate side effect of feeling their emotions—all of them, all at once. Since she was six, Sarah had to learn how block them out or risk going mad. It was a constant effort and drain on her energy.

Except for when she was around Grayle.

The boy projected some kind of dampening field, making any nearby auras fade away. It happened every time she got close to him—in the hallways, school cafeteria, the Roman exhibit five minutes ago.

She focused on his void now, trying to flush him out in the crowd.

I let myself get distracted for a second and now he's—

She sensed an emptiness ahead, a dark pocket among the glowing auras.

There.

She spotted Grayle standing next to a series of velvet cordons. Stopping a few feet behind, Sarah pretended to join onlookers craning their necks to catch a glimpse of the city's rich, powerful, and famous parading down a carpet runner bisecting the room. Among them was the mayor of Vancouver, star hockey players, a famous French-Canadian actress, and a ditsy heiress with a chihuahua in her handbag.

Sarah froze, recognizing the next man. Sebastian Caine, a British entrepreneur said to be worth billions. He walked tall and deliberate, like a man overcome with his own self-importance. He looked maybe fifty years old with a neatly trimmed goatee and longish white hair tied into a ponytail. His eyes were hidden behind dark sunglasses. He wore a tailored black tuxedo, a white shirt, and silver bow tie. His wingtip shoes sparkled like mirrors as he made his way past reporters, ignoring their requests for an interview. Sarah had only read about him in mission briefings, the man responsible for the deaths of at least three of her kind... including her mother. Here was the proof that he wasn't just a figure conjured up in her nightmares.

He was real.

Following half a step behind lumbered Caine's seven-foot, three-hundred-pound bodyguard, Nils Mussels. The man's bulk threatened to burst through his tuxedo. His beady eyes, half hidden under a sloping brow, studied the crowd for signs of trouble.

Anger coursed through Sarah, bubbling just beneath the surface.

She was so close. With one little flick of her wrist, with one little spell, she'd be able to—

"You impressed?"

Sarah jumped as Alistair Thorn's warm aura sidled next to her. She never felt him coming. Her supernatural senses clouded whenever she got too scared or angry. "Impressed with these celebrities?" she said. "I hardly think so."

She looked up at him. His gorgeous, dark brown eyes studied her.

"You're not even looking forward to seeing Jameson Blaze?" he asked.

"Especially not Jameson Blaze," Sarah said. She knew he was teasing. They'd been doing a flirting tango back and forth since Sarah arrived at Bayview three weeks ago.

One side of Alistair's mouth pulled up into a smile. "I can tell you're going to be a tough girl to impress."

Sarah turned away. It was hard enough to focus on the mission for the next twenty minutes without Alistair's serious good looks distracting her. She liked him—more than a little. But she couldn't afford the complications of a relationship. Her missions prevented such things. Enter, integrate, complete the job—all without developing personal attachments.

After today, I'll never see him again anyway.

Pandemonium erupted outside. Sarah could see fans shouting and waving their signs through the museum's tinted windows.

"I bet Blaze just showed up," Alistair said. He used his body to protect her as more reporters and photographers shoved by.

Cute, Sarah thought. *He thinks I need protecting.* If he knew what she could do, he'd be asking for *her* protection, not the other way around. But Sarah pressed against his chest anyway, taking in his warmth and the smell of his cologne.

Security personnel opened the outside doors to a flurry of camera flashes announcing the pop star's arrival.

Jameson Blaze waved and blew kisses to the crowd, soaking up their affection. They swooned over his smile, light-blue eyes, and mop haircut. Even Sarah had to admit Blaze was cute, in that cocky I'm-a-rock-star kind of way. At sixteen, he was the world's latest singing sensation, having climbed the charts with a string of popular hits and then, naturally, coming out with his own line of clothing—J. Blay Bling.

Sarah watched her classmates lose their minds. Tears streamed down their cheeks. "Jameson, we love you!" they screamed. If Sarah didn't know better, she would have thought J. Blay was giving off an infatuation spell. Just to be sure, she let her guard down, allowing the auras to magnify around her again. The pop star shimmered yellow with a slight purplish tinge she'd learned to associate with artistically talented Outlanders. But she was confident he didn't possess any magical abilities.

Blaze arrived in the VIP seating area in front of the stage just as Sebastian Caine made his way onto the podium. Miss Jennings nervously straightened her uniform. She shook his hand vigorously, babbling something the rest of the audience couldn't hear. Caine laughed at whatever she had to say—it looked fake.

Caine moved behind the lectern and gave a final wave. "Thank you, everyone, for coming. This is a wonderful occasion," he said into the microphone, hushing girls still tittering about J. Blay. His English accent sounded confident, a voice that was used to giving orders. "The Vancouver Museum is an important part of our great city's heritage. It has been a pleasure to do my part in seeing its renovations completed. But we must give credit to where credit is due. If it weren't for the tireless efforts of Alberic Clement, the new Vancouver Museum would never have been accomplished. So, without further delay, let me be the first to congratulate Mr. Clement."

An elderly man in the front row rose shakily to his feet. Alberic Clement was thin, relying on a cane to keep from tipping over. His black tuxedo might have fit him once but now hung loose on his withered frame.

The crowd cheered. Even the Bayview students seemed caught up in the moment, although Sarah was sure they had no idea who Clement was. According to her research, Alberic Clement was a local businessman and collector of rare antiquities but, unlike Caine, had no suspicious dealings in his past… that she knew of.

A tour guide helped the old man onto the podium where Caine waited.

The two men shook hands and Clement settled behind the podium. "Before we officially open the Vancouver Museum and its newest exhibit," his scratchy voice echoed, "let me tell you about my vision for this institution—"

Without warning, the crazed J. Blay fans outside surged forward, pressing against the museum's doors. The tinted glass threatened to shatter under the pressure. Police officers hurried to barricade the entrance with their bodies. Security personnel raced to help, leaving their posts unguarded.

Sarah felt rather than saw Grayle moving off. When she looked back, both he and his void had disappeared.

Chapter 3

Grayle saw his chance. With everyone's attention fixed on the museum's entrance, he ducked under the velvet rope and rushed across the red carpet, disappearing into the sea of spectators on the other side. Pushing past his classmates, he reached the medieval exhibit unnoticed and made his way past suits of armor, weapons, and tapestries. Like any good thief, he'd cased out the museum's schematics, committing its layout to memory. He turned another corner and entered a room filled with exquisite art and painted frescoes from all corners of the ancient world. The room was a dead end, or so it appeared. Grayle headed for a dark curtain hanging at the far end and pushed it aside, revealing a hidden metal door. He stepped inside and closed the curtain behind him.

He took out his phone and quickly tapped a message to Zito: "About to enter exhibit. Need description of item."

He waited for a reply.

Nothing came.

The curtain suddenly swished open. The blood drained from Grayle's face so fast he thought he'd pass out.

"Hurry, get us in," Sarah said, yanking the curtain shut again. "I think a guard followed me."

"What the hell are you doing here?" Grayle hissed.

Before she could answer, the crackle of a radio and approaching footsteps confirmed her suspicion. Someone else was in the room.

"I thought I saw a kid going into the medieval exhibit," a gravelly voice said from the opposite side of the curtain. "I'm checking it out. Over." The radio chirped off.

Flying into motion, Grayle slid his hands around the doorframe, getting on his toes to reach the topmost edge.

Nothing—no wires disguising hidden trip sensors.

He rifled through his coat pocket and removed his student ID card from his wallet. Grayle wedged the card into the doorjamb, jiggling it between the lock and frame. Applying just the right amount of pressure, he was rewarded with a faint click. The door opened and they quickly slipped inside. No sooner had Grayle gently closed the door behind them than he heard the curtain being whipped aside and footsteps coming closer.

The door rattled.

Grayle held his breath.

"Must have been a false alarm." The guard's voice was just inches away. "I'm heading back, over."

Grayle waited until the guard had left then spun to face Sarah. "What the hell are you doing here?" he asked again.

"Wanted to see what you were up to," Sarah whispered. "Quick. Follow me. Watch your step."

They were in an empty emergency stairwell. It appeared neglected, compared to the rest of the renovated museum. Cracks marred the exposed brick walls, and paint peeled from wooden banisters. Some stairs were in such horrible disrepair Grayle doubted they would support his weight.

"You're not supposed to be here," he said, climbing after her.

"Neither are you."

Reaching the topmost landing, Sarah stopped in front of another metal door. "This is it," she said, stepping aside to let Grayle pass.

He turned the handle. It was unlocked.

His caution leapt into overdrive. *Something isn't right.* He opened the door, half expecting alarms to go off and SWAT teams to rappel from the ceiling.

Sarah squeezed by him.

Grayle hung back, not sure what to do next. He'd never broken into a place with someone else tagging along. His instincts told him to abandon the job and take whatever consequences Zito decided to hand out.

Sarah poked her head through the doorway and arched an eyebrow. "What are you waiting for?"

Despite his better judgment, Grayle followed.

They entered another area sectioned off by black curtains. Grayle peeked through the velvet drapes. A shaft of daylight angled down through a skylight in the ceiling. He scanned the room for motion sensors and security cameras. They had been in every other exhibit, red lights blinking away in dark corners, but security in this part of the museum seemed non-existent— no guards, cameras, laser sensors, light detectors, body heat sensors—nothing.

He peered over his shoulder. Sarah stared back at him expectantly.

What am I going to do? He knew none of the security

measures would affect him, but Sarah complicated matters. He slipped his backpack off his shoulder and grabbed her hand. It felt soft and warm. She didn't pull away as he expected her to.

"Stay close. No talking," he said, leading her to a railing overlooking the exhibit. A partially complete replica of a Viking longship dominated the ground floor. The ship measured nearly forty feet from bow to stern, wider in the middle and tapering off at each end. An elaborately carved dragon head loomed from the prow and shields decorated one edge where Viking oarsmen would have sat, paddling upriver, plundering villages and monasteries along the way. With only pieces of wooden planks thrusting upright like skeletal ribs, the ship looked more like a horrible beast that had dragged itself from the sea than an archaeological discovery.

Still holding hands, Grayle led Sarah down a long ramp curving to the ground floor. New carpet cushioned their steps. They passed display cases arrayed with all manner of weapons: broad-bladed axes, spears, and longswords. The scent of pinewood and glass cleaner drifted throughout the room.

Reaching the main floor, Grayle let go of Sarah's hand. He watched her ogle one glass case after another as though she were window-shopping. She stopped at what looked like a large stone glinting softly behind polished glass.

He came up beside her and read the caption on a brass plaque fastened to the casing.

RUNESTONE circa 1098 C.E.
Runestone found near Hammerfest in northern Norway.
On loan to the Vancouver Museum by an anonymous donor.

"This is it, but… " She knit her eyebrows.
"But what?"

"It's on loan by an anonymous donor," she said. "That can't be right."

"What's so strange about that?"

"It's supposed to belong to Sebastian Caine."

"Why? Who cares who it belongs—"

Thump. Thump. Thump.

Screams and loud applause erupted outside the exhibit's doors. Clement must have introduced Jameson Blaze to the stage. A heavy, rhythmic bass began pumping out the star's latest hit.

How much time do I have left before the doors swing open? Ten minutes, maybe less?

His phone buzzed. A message from Zito: "Intended object is a Viking runestone fragment. Get it now."

Is he kidding? This thing must weigh like a hundred pounds. Grayle desperately scanned the exhibit for a smaller runestone, one that could actually be carried out without him having to turn into the Incredible Hulk. *I'll never be able to get it out of here, especially with Miss Curious tagging along.*

Kneeling on one knee, he examined the stone closer. It was black in color except for greenish hues in areas where light reflected off its smooth surface. Carvings of what looked like letters were submerged beneath its shiny surface.

"Those are runes, an old form of Viking writing," Sarah explained. "Vikings celebrated their bravery and victories in battle with memorial stones. Archaeologists call them runestones."

"It looks like these letters were somehow chiselled beneath its surface. How's that possible?" Grayle asked, searching for the display case's security wiring and pressure plates.

"Not sure," she said. Sarah took out a smartphone from her pink bag and aimed it at the stone.

"Whoa… what are you doing?"

"What does it look like? Taking pictures."

Trying to back away, Grayle lost his balance and braced himself against the glass. As if charged by his proximity, the stone's inscriptions began to glow. New runes appeared, previously hidden from the naked eye, bleeding into the empty spaces between the visible letters and rough design bordering the fragment.

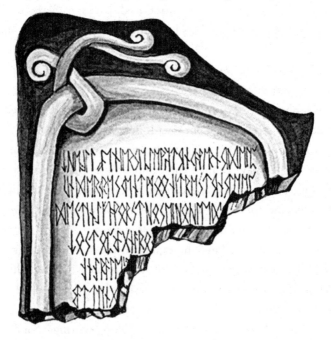

"How are you doing that?" Sarah asked.

Grayle took his hand off the glass. The glowing letters melted away. He touched the glass again, and the etchings reappeared.

Definitely me. I'm doing this—but how? "Maybe they're sensitive to body heat or something," he said.

Sarah stared at the stone and snapped more photos.

"I wonder what they say," Grayle said.

"Can't be sure, but some of it talks about—"

"You can read that?"

She nodded. "It says—" Sarah stopped abruptly and jerked her head from side to side. "Do you smell something?" she asked.

Grayle crinkled his nose. "Yeah. What is that?" It smelled like a science experiment he'd done in chemistry class last semester, mixing acid with another compound to make something that smelled like rotten eggs.

"It's brimstone," Sarah said.

"Brimstone?"

"Sulphur." Her movements suddenly became more alert. She panned the room, her gaze finally stopping at the exhibit's ceiling. "Are the skylights connected to the security system?"

"Nothing's connected," Grayle said a little too quickly. He hoped she wouldn't ask him how he knew.

Without warning, Sarah grabbed his arm and pulled him behind a different display case a few feet away.

"What're you—" Grayle tried to shake free from her grip. She was surprisingly strong.

Sarah squeezed harder, silencing him. "Don't ask," she warned, her face half hidden in shadow.

"What do you mean *don't ask*? I need to—"

"Shhh. There's some*thing* in here with us."

Chapter 4

Grayle saw something slide beyond the Viking longship, appearing and disappearing, keeping to the far edges of the exhibit.

"Don't move," Sarah whispered, turning on her cell phone. She covered the LED display as it gleamed in the darkness. "Damn. No signal."

"I'm not sticking around to get caught," Grayle whispered. "I'm outta here."

"Stay put," Sarah hissed, yanking him down and almost tearing his sleeve off.

He was about to protest when a shapeless form glided along the longship's portside.

Grayle's heart pounded. Were the dark and shadows playing tricks on him? The intruder, whoever it was, seemed to shift and blend with the darkness until it solidified into a figure dressed in a flowing black cloak. The cloak's hem gently rose and fell as though floating in some gentle, invisible current. The figure removed its cowl. Grayle stared at the stunning face of a woman with blond hair and a flawless, milky white complexion.

"Who is that?" he asked.

"Hel, the goddess of death," Sarah whispered.

Goddess? Grayle nearly burst out laughing. But when he turned to look at Sarah, the color had washed from her face. It wasn't a joke. As ridiculous as it seemed, *she* believed it was the truth.

"Then let's get out of here," he said.

"No." Her voice was shaky but determined. "We need to see what she's up to."

The goddess, or whoever it was, glided along the longship, focusing on the shields surrounding its outer edge. Scanning each one, she drifted closer to their hiding place, stopping only a few feet away.

The sulphur smell intensified, stinging Grayle's eyes. He stifled a cough and blinked away tears.

Apparently not finding what she was searching for, the goddess turned and panned the rest of the exhibit. She spied the glass case containing the runestone.

Sarah turned to Grayle, put a finger to her lips, and slipped behind another display case a few feet closer. He followed, sidling up beside her.

From there, they watched Hel extend her arms toward the stone. Silver gauntlets covered the goddess's hands and forearms. Elaborate designs carved on their surface glinted in the low light.

In a whisper, sounding both close and distant all at once, the goddess chanted in a language Grayle had never heard. No sooner had she uttered the words than the stone fragment loosened from its clamps and passed *through* the casing without breaking the surrounding glass. Hel's lips parted in a triumphant smile. The runestone hovered inches from her waiting hands.

"Get away from that!" Sarah yelled, jumping out from their hiding place.

The stone thudded onto the carpet and tipped on its side.

The two faced off like desperados in a gunfight. Sarah moved into a fighting stance. Her hands trembled.

Grayle watched the goddess's eyes glow a harsh neon green. They narrowed maliciously, a look he'd seen a dozen times when foster parents punished him, principals expelled him, and the courts sentenced him to eighteen months at Gloomshroud.

He tried to warn Sarah but couldn't get his mouth to form the words. He lunged instead, knocking her out of the way as a blinding flash launched from the goddess's gauntlets. Whatever it was skimmed Grayle's waist, sending them both crashing through a display case containing a mannequin wearing Viking armor and weapons.

Glass rained down on them like a thousand diamonds.

Grayle got up slowly, clutching his ribs. Glass crunched under his shoes.

Sarah stirred a few feet away. A trickle of blood ran down her forehead.

Hel glided toward her.

It was more a reflex than a conscious action. Grayle scooped up a sword from the shattered display case and, ignoring the protest from his ribs, covered the space between him and Hel in an instant. He stood between the goddess and Sarah, holding the sword with both hands at Hel's chest.

"Don't come any closer," he warned. The sword's weight strained the muscles in his wrists and forearms.

Hel did the last thing he expected. With a screech of metal on metal, she grabbed the blade in both gauntlets. Grayle tugged, trying to loose the weapon from her grip.

Hel smiled, and to Grayle's horror, her face began to change. It morphed so that one side remained the beautiful woman he'd first seen, but her left half fell away. The skin and the muscle tissue underneath flaked off like leaves blown away in a wind. What was left was half a skull, bleached white and menacing.

Grayle gasped.

Hel ripped the sword from his hands and tossed it aside.

Defenceless, Grayle stumbled back—horrified by the goddess's hideous form.

Her eyes smouldered a sickly neon green. The designs covering her gauntlets began to glow, charging with power. A bolt, greater than the one before, discharged, forking in Grayle's direction.

This time, he couldn't dodge it fast enough.

Chapter 5

Sarah screamed as the lightning hit Grayle square in the chest, scattering into smaller bolts and shattering the display cases around him. All she wanted was for him to get her into the exhibit—there wasn't supposed to be a confrontation with a goddess—nobody was supposed to die. But as the smoke cleared, her horror turned to amazement. Grayle stood unharmed amidst smoking debris and blackened walls. A charred hole in his jacket was the only evidence that Hel's dark magic had struck him.

Sarah didn't have time to figure out how he was able to survive the attack. She had no time to think at all, other than how to escape this place with the runestone and their lives.

She spotted an object on the wall—a fire alarm. She ran to it and smashed the security glass.

"No… don't!" Grayle shouted.

Too late. She'd already pulled the switch.

Sirens wailed, and emergency lights flared.

"You shouldn't have done that," Grayle yelled over the noise. He leaned against the wall, slipping off what was left of his smoldering jacket, letting it drop to the floor.

Sarah stumbled across the exhibit. Blood seeped from a cut along her hairline. "What are you talking about? If I didn't, we would've—"

She was interrupted by a low rumbling sound and mechanical hisses coming from vents along the ceiling. Metal security shutters started inching down over the exit doors and skylights.

"Okay. That can't be good," she admitted.

"We have to get out of here before we're trapped inside," Grayle warned. "C'mon."

"No! Not without the runestone."

"Forget the stone."

She couldn't. The fragment was a piece of a larger puzzle. Even if it wasn't the runestone her mother had searched for, she couldn't let Hel take it.

Sarah ran to where the artifact rested on the carpet. Hel materialized in a plume of shadow and smoke, blocking her path. She crossed her arms over her head and splayed her fingers. Whispering in the same mystical language as before, the shields fastened along the longship's railing suddenly rattled like dinner plates in a cabinet. One by one, they shook free, swooping down and spinning over the goddess's head.

This is bad. Sarah scanned the room, searching desperately for anything she could use as a weapon. She spied another shield lying on the floor twenty feet away.

Despite strict rules forbidding witches from using their powers in the presence of Outlanders, she had to use her magic.

Breaking rules is better than being dead.

She shouted her retrieval spell. "Toltha!" The shield shuddered, then flew through the air and into her waiting hand.

"How did you—" Grayle began.

Before he could finish, the goddess's gauntlets clapped together with a loud metallic clang. The shields floating above her head hurtled toward them.

Sarah glimpsed Grayle in her peripheral vision, throwing himself behind a display case as the first flying disc nearly took his head off. She gripped her new shield tight to her body. Hel's next two shields bashed against it, deflecting in different directions and smashing display cases across the room. Another disc skidded along the floor. Like a stone skipping on water, it slammed into Sarah's ankle, tripping her painfully to the floor. She cried out, still trying to keep her shield between her and Hel.

Three shields remained, hovering over the goddess like mini flying saucers.

Sarah got up. The throbbing in her ankle only added to her resolve. "I will not let you leave here with the stone," she said, letting her anger stoke the magic inside her. Blue energy ignited around her hands.

Hel didn't answer. Her half-human lips twisted into a cruel smile. She let loose the last three shields, hurling them in Sarah's direction.

"Vanya!" Sarah flung her magic. It shot like a pulse wave from her hands, deflecting all three shields harmlessly out of the way.

Hel glanced up at the closing skylights then back at Sarah. She thrust an arm toward the runestone, lying a few yards away. Smoke swirled from her fingers, curling around the fragment like a coiling serpent.

"No!"

Sarah moved to intervene, but the goddess conjured a cyclone from her gauntlets. The magic windstorm grew in intensity, raging across the room. The longship's sails whipped and snapped. Shattered glass and broken artifacts swirled everywhere. Sarah ducked behind her shield to keep from being pelted by debris.

Enveloped in her own whirlwind, Hel jetted toward the ceiling. She and the runestone dissipated into a cloud of smoke and seeped through a crack of open skylight just as the metal shutters clanked shut.

✳ ✳ ✳

Grayle had curled into a ball as the floating debris caught in the goddess's wake crashed around him. Chunks of marble bombarded his body, and a spear sliced into the carpet inches from his head.

He'd lost sight of Sarah after she somehow made a shield fly into her hand.

Who is this girl? How was she able to do that?

He shoved the questions aside for now. The alarms and hissing vents reminded him getting out of there was more urgent. He got up from behind the crumbling display case and scanned what was left of the exhibit. The room was in shambles. Apart from the Viking ship still rooted on its struts, pieces of glass, marble, and priceless artifacts littered the floor.

He spotted Sarah kneeling a few feet away, shoulders slumped. The shield hung loosely from her forearm.

"C'mon," he shouted above the sirens. "Everything's sealing itself shut."

She didn't move.

"Sarah! The oxygen's being pumped out. Part of the museum's new fire-prevention measures. If we don't get out now, we never will."

She slung the shield's strap over her shoulder and slowly rose to her feet. Off balance, she stumbled to the side, but Grayle caught her around the waist. Together, they rushed up the winding ramp.

"How can they shut the exits and vent the air when there are still people inside?" she asked, hobbling next to him.

"There isn't supposed to be anyone in here, remember? There would've been enough time to get out if we didn't have to fight off that goddess thing."

They made it to the curtain. Grayle whipped it aside, set Sarah gently on the carpet, and headed for the door. "Ah, crap." Another metal shutter covered the stairwell exit.

Sarah slipped the shield off her shoulder and reached for her pink bag. She zipped it open and took out a laptop. "See that panel?" she said, pointing to a state-of-the-art number pad next to the door. "I need you to open the cover."

"Sure. Happen to have a screwdriver?" Grayle asked sarcastically. "Why don't you..." he hesitated, still trying to come to grips with how she managed to get a shield to fly into her hand. "Why don't you hocus pocus our way out?"

"I can't." She plugged a USB cable into the laptop. "The shutters, doors, and panels are made of iron. Magic won't work on iron."

"Magic won't... When we get out of here, you've got some explaining to do." Grayle moved toward her. "Here, give me that."

She handed him the laptop.

"Not that. That!" He pointed to the shield.

Scrunching her face, she passed it to him. "But we need to hack the keypad's com—"

Grayle slammed the edge of the shield into the wall.

"—bination," Sarah finished.

He turned the shield at a different angle and smashed the wall again a foot beneath the number pad.

"What are you doing?" Sarah asked.

"This is a Briggs & Frommer security keypad," Grayle wheezed. The air was getting thinner by the second. "It has a failsafe to prevent direct hacking... new feature. But I might be able to override the door's mechanism if I can access its wiring."

He swung the shield one last time. With a crunch, he pounded a small triangular gap in the wall. He knelt down and picked away at the remaining drywall, exposing the panel's wiring. The effort of creating the hole, combined with the lack of air, was rapidly depleting his strength.

Loud banging echoed from the exhibit's main entrance below. Security was trying to force their way in.

Why don't they just shut down the safety protocols? Grayle thought. He was afraid by the time that happened, he'd be passed out.

He peered inside the hole he'd created, his vision blurring. Five wires, blue, red, yellow, green, and white, wound their way down a center pole. Grayle gritted his teeth, recognizing the tangle of lead, ground and dummy wires.

"I don't suppose you have a knife or—"

"Will nail clippers work?" Sarah was already digging in her bag. "Here."

He took the clippers and reached for the wires. He hesitated.

"What is it? Why are you stopping?"

Grayle held up a finger, signalling her to be quiet. His palms were slick with sweat. He needed to focus. Each wire had to be cut in the proper sequence. Cut the wrong one and the door's mechanism would shut down, trapping them inside for good.

The hand holding the clippers trembled.

Slow down. Have to do this right.

He took a deep breath. Using his right hand to steady the left, Grayle snipped the white wire then the yellow. The tips of his fingers tingled, going numb. He cut the red, the blue, and finally the green wire.

The failsafes remained intact.

Next, he needed to cross-connect the right wires.

Which ones were they again?

"Blue and yellow or blue and red?" he mumbled.

Sarah crawled next to him. "What? Can't you do it?"

Grayle tuned her out.

Blue. Red. Yellow. Green. White.

He started seeing spots.

More banging echoed downstairs.

Blue. Red. Yellow. Green. White. Wait... blue feeds the main power through the circuit board and...

Careful not to electrocute himself, he reached inside and stopped. He saw three of the same wire shifting in and out of focus. The tingling prickled over his entire body and face. He was going to pass out.

With his last ounce of focus, he crossed the blue and white wires.

The world spun. Grayle could feel Sarah frantically shaking him, calling out his name. But he was already drifting, letting the peaceful darkness fold over him and lull him to sleep.

Chapter 6

The recurring nightmare came to Grayle more vividly than ever before. It always started the same way, taking him back five years—to the day of his first memory.

He remembered standing in a forest, cold darkness bleeding over his skin. His breath puffed foggy white in the chilly air—slowly at first, then faster as panic set in.

He was stranded.

Alone.

He peered over his shoulder and saw the full moon casting its reflection off a nearby lake. The water rippled. Rings flowed ever wider until they faded along the frosty shoreline. Then the surface grew still, like a mirror.

City lights peeked through the trees. Distant traffic noise reached him.

Where am I?

His little legs felt numb and his head groggy, as if he'd just woken from a deep sleep. Dampness hung in the air, curling through the folds of his clothing. He looked down. His shirt was tattered, his jeans dirty at the knees, and his sneakers soaked and filthy, as if he'd been running through mud. His hands were wet and sticky, splotched with ruby patches that glistened in the moonlight.

Blood.

He frantically wiped his palms on his shirt but only succeeded in staining the white cotton a dark crimson.

What's happened?

Piercing the silence, two crows cawed somewhere high in the forest canopy. A prickling sensation raced up Grayle's spine. He felt as if something or someone was staring at him from the darkness. He heard rustling. A twig snapped close by, followed by a low groan.

He wasn't alone.

Whatever lurked in the shadows spurred some primal instinct. Grayle stumbled through the woods, the bark scraping his hands as he braced himself from tree to tree. Wet pine needles slapped his face, and cones crunched beneath his feet. His shoes slipped in the frosty undergrowth, sending him sprawling. There he lay, spent and shivering, smelling wet leaves in his nostrils and listening to the frantic thumping of his heartbeat

There it was again—more rustling from the bushes off to his right.

Grayle turned to look. He glimpsed a gangly figure silhouetted by moonlight limping toward him, dragging a leg behind itself like heavy luggage. Despite its awkward pace, the creature moved steadily closer. For a moment, it got tangled in brush and low-hanging branches. Twisting and writhing, the creature loosened one arm then the other. Soon it would be free.

Grayle lay frozen, unable to move or tear his eyes away. He felt a tug on his arm and the sensation of being dragged. Fresh oxygen filled his lungs.

His eyes snapped open. He drew in several gasping breaths. His vision was blinded by a piercing fluorescent light, blotted out a second later by a dark shape.

Sarah.

He was back in the museum.

Her hair hung down, black strands of silk, tickling his nose as she examined him. Her lips moved, but the sounds were muffled. Gradually, her hazy image and voice sharpened.

"Hey, you okay?" She put her hand on his chest.

Grayle sat up, holding his head. "Yeah, I think so."

"You sure? Looked like you were having a nightmare."

He shrugged off her concern, but the lingering memories weren't so easy to dismiss. Sure, he'd had the dream—nightmare, whatever—before, but never so vividly. He could still feel the cold surrounding him and the smell of wet pine needles. The creature was about to get loose—*but what happened after that?* He could never remember.

He pushed the memories aside. "Where are we?"

She offered him a hand. He grabbed her forearm and got to his feet. "We're back in the stairwell. You passed out just when you disabled the door's security. I pulled you through before the air ran out."

The door to the exhibit was still open. Alarms blared, and shouts echoed from somewhere deep inside.

"C'mon, before they figure out where we went." Sarah shouldered her bag and the shield she'd used to defend herself against the goddess.

"You should leave that here," Grayle said, nodding toward the shield.

She gave him a bewildered look. "It might come in handy again."

"But if we're caught, they'll know we stole it."

"Only *if* we get caught."

"But look at the size of it!"

A shadow fell over the landing before Sarah could answer. Grayle's heart leapt to his throat. At first, he thought it belonged to Hel coming back to finish them off. Then he recognized the shadow's wiry frame.

"You runt!" Zito barked. "I knew you'd screw this up."

Grayle tensed. "How'd you get in here?"

"Never mind that. Where's the runestone?" The foster parent searched Grayle's hands and the landing floor.

"How did you expect me to get a hundred-pound stone out of here?" Grayle snapped.

Zito went bug-eye. "Do you realize what you've done? You've ruined my biggest score!"

"I didn't count on a—"

But Zito wasn't listening. He howled his outrage and, with his hands outstretched and fingers curled like claws, lunged at Grayle.

Sarah shouted, "Vanya!" and the same invisible force Grayle had seen her use to deflect Hel's spinning shields knocked the foster parent clear across the landing. His body crashed into the guard rail.

Stunned for only a moment, Zito's face twisted into an ugly snarl. He charged again, this time at Sarah.

With split-second reflexes, Grayle kicked the edge of Sarah's shield up like a skateboard. Flipping it in front of him, he rushed headlong at his foster parent and rammed him clear through the open exhibit door.

Sarah snatched Grayle by the collar and pulled him out before slamming the door shut. Clicking twice, the door's locking mechanisms reinitialized, trapping Zito inside the exhibit.

Sarah cradled her hand. Touching the iron had sizzled her skin. "I take it that was your foster parent," she said, wincing.

Zito's muffled threats could be heard from behind the door. "I'll kill you, boy. If it's the last thing I do, I'll make you pay for this!"

Grayle dropped the shield on the landing. "Yeah, um... he doesn't really like me."

"I kinda noticed that."

"He'll try to pin the runestone's theft on me," Grayle said.

"Then the best thing to do is get out of here." Sarah knelt down and hovered her hands inches above the shield. A blue flash appeared in the space between her fingers and its wood and bronze surface. Almost instantly, the shield shrank to the size of a Frisbee. "Let's go," she said, easily fitting the shield into her bag.

"Who or *what* are you?" Grayle asked.

She was already limping down the stairwell. "No time to explain," she yelled.

Grayle didn't know what to do. Did he really want to follow her? A part of him wanted to go it alone, maybe even turn himself in—prove it wasn't him who stole the runestone. For the first time, he'd be telling the truth—and it was probably the simpler, smarter course of action.

When have I ever done the simple or smart thing?

Zito thumped on the door, keeping up a steady stream of curses.

Grayle sighed, grabbed his backpack, and chased after Sarah. Wooden planks creaked and groaned beneath him as he spiralled toward the ground floor. An emergency exit had been pried open. He caught up to Sarah and, together, they burst into the cool air outside.

Chapter 7

Sebastian Caine watched the chaos unfold around him.

Police officers hustled in and out of rooms, scouring the museum for whoever had left the Viking exhibit in ruins. Their walkie-talkies crackled on and off in succession as teams combed each floor. Firefighters and medical personnel tended to guests traumatized after the alarm swept panic through the rotunda, causing a rampage for the exits.

Paramedics were busy fitting an oxygen mask over one of the invited actresses. She breathed in deeply, an arm draped dramatically over her forehead. Caine wasn't sure whether she was really in distress or simply providing a show for the paparazzi. Any publicity was good publicity for an actress wishing to stay in the limelight.

For Caine, however, bad publicity was a fact of life. No doubt CNN and the other major television networks were already searching for ways to smear his name, linking today's events to other questionable incidences involving him and his global enterprise.

So be it—a bad reputation didn't bother him.

Failing to capture a witch did.

He cursed himself for focusing too much on trapping her and not taking the stone fragment when he had the chance. He'd been unaware of the fragment's existence until it was secured in its display case. He could have switched it with a fake easily enough. But, in order to lure a witch, only a true Folklorian artifact could be used as bait.

"I'm telling you it was him, I'm sure of it!" A balding man with a long, sharp nose ranted to a nearby constable. A group of teenagers sat scattered on the floor around them. "That boy's been nothing but trouble."

"And you haven't seen him since the alarms went off, Mr. Snodgrass?" asked the young officer. He pushed his hat higher on his forehead and pulled out a notepad.

Snodgrass shook his head. "He and another student, Sarah Finn, disappeared before all this happened. One minute, I saw them in the rotunda, the next minute they were gone." He watched the officer scribble and didn't speak again until the pen came to a stop. "The boy has a history of crime and violence. I'm sure he's involved in this somehow…"

Looking past the constable, Caine saw two officers ushering a wiry-looking man in handcuffs discreetly toward a rear exit. It was Sylvester Zito—the freelance thief he'd hired to steal the runestone. Caine's lips pressed together. Another failure. Luckily, the man didn't know the identity of his true employer. Caine couldn't be implicated. They disappeared through a side exit before Caine could follow.

His attention shifted again, this time to reporters descending on Alberic Clement. The old man had stupidly ventured past the police tape erected around the entrance to the Viking exhibit, making him fair game for the members of the press lurking just beyond. They thrust microphones in his face and shouted questions all at once. The old man shielded his eyes and backed away.

Caine ducked under the police tape and squeezed between him and the reporters. "Ladies and gentlemen," he said, raising his hands in a gesture for calm. "On behalf of Mr. Clement, I am shocked and truly saddened at what has transpired here today." His practiced voice remained even. "Mr. Clement has contributed priceless artifacts from his own private collection. I assure you, we will discover who the perpetrators are and make sure justice is served." Caine spotted a police inspector wearing a brown overcoat making his way through the crowd. "And if the police are unable to do anything," he continued, "then I will place the extensive resources of Caine Enterprises at Mr. Clement's disposal. After all, he is one of our city's most generous philanthropists, and deserves to have his collection recovered."

"Excuse me." The inspector pushed past the last row of reporters. He had unkempt brown hair, greying over his ears, and a walrus-like moustache that covered his upper lip.

Caine moved aside, letting the inspector replace him at Clement's side.

A redheaded reporter with too much pink lipstick thrust a microphone in the inspector's face. "Inspector Timmins, considering the upgrades to the museum's security, how is it possible that items were stolen from the Viking exhibit?"

Caine suppressed a grin. How could the police know he'd arranged to have the exhibit's security measures switched off? You can't capture a witch and let the whole world know about it. Yet the alarms went off anyway, and despite Caine having ensured all means of escape were covered in iron, his "contributions" to the museum's renovations, whoever had been in the exhibit still got away.

"Ladies and gentlemen," Timmins said gruffly. "Considerable damage was done to the Viking exhibit. Our preliminary findings suggest this was a targeted theft. The thieves knew exactly what they were looking for. Our investigators are currently trying to ascertain how the items were taken from the exhibit. We have one suspect in custody but have reason to believe there may have been others involved."

Caine's face twitched. *Others?*

"We are talking to witnesses and taking statements," the inspector continued. "Rest assured, the Vancouver Police Department is doing everything possible to return these stolen items to Mr. Clement and apprehend the culprits responsible for this heinous crime."

"Can you describe the artifacts taken?" asked the redheaded reporter.

"Who is the man you have in custody? How do you know he had accomplices?" shouted a photographer wearing an NBC ball cap.

Before Timmins could answer, a uniformed officer broke through the crowd, the same one who had interviewed Snodgrass. He whispered something in the inspector's ear. Timmins knit his bushy eyebrows and gave the officer a quick nod. "If you'll excuse me, our investigation continues. As soon as we have more facts, we'll make them available to the press." He turned and passed under the police tape, ignoring any further questions.

With the inspector gone, the reporters swooped on Clement again.

Caine didn't care. He left the old man to fend for himself and followed Timmins and the constable. He leaned against a concrete column, pretending to check his smartphone for messages as the two men spoke.

"What is it?" he overheard Timmins say.

The young officer bristled with excitement. "We found this among the rubble at the crime scene." He held up a charred jacket; holes had burned through the pleather fabric. He produced a wallet buried inside a pocket and handed it to Timmins.

"Grayle Rowen."

"That's one of the missing students," the officer said with a satisfied smile, "and he has a criminal record." He handed the inspector his notepad. "There's no picture, but I got a description from his teacher."

Timmins smiled, scanning the information. "Looks like we may have found our accomplice, if not the thief himself." He closed the notepad and gave back the wallet. "Put out an APB for Grayle Rowen: age fifteen, five foot ten, slim build, gray eyes, and brown hair. He'll be walking without a jacket and possibly with a girl the same age. Go."

The constable hurried off.

Caine did the same, weaving past the students, celebrities, and emergency personnel remaining in the rotunda. He pushed through the swinging doors leading into the cafeteria's kitchen.

Nils Mussels waited near the back exit. He threw what was left of a triple-stacked sandwich onto the counter and held open Caine's coat. A thick glob of mustard stained the bodyguard's mouth. At seven feet and three hundred pounds, he needed a steady stream of calories to maintain his intimidating size.

"Do you have the security footage?" Caine asked, slipping his arms into his jacket.

"*Oui*, chef," the bodyguard answered and held up a small SD card.

"Good. We don't have a moment to spare."

Mussels opened the exit door and led the way to a waiting stretched Hummer limousine. He opened the rear door for Caine then went around to the opposite side. The vehicle's suspension strained as he folded his giant frame inside and shut the door behind him.

The Hummer was an impressive vehicle. The outer shell and windows were comprised of dense ballistic glass and steel, making the vehicle virtually impenetrable. Even the undercarriage was reinforced with titanium plating—not even a land mine could pierce it. For added measure, Caine had demanded iron strips be layered in the Hummer's frame to protect him from supernatural attacks. One could never be too careful.

But however impressive the vehicle was on the outside, it was even more remarkable within. Plush white leather seats and a bar lined one side of the interior while computer consoles, linked to Caine's communications satellite in orbit, covered the length of the other. From inside the vehicle, he had unrestricted access to his entire global enterprise, not to mention a worldwide intelligence network that rivalled both Britain's MI6 or the CIA.

Caine pressed an intercom switch. "Caine Tower," he directed the limo driver.

The Hummer sped away from the throng of reporters, flashing lights, and news vans outside the museum.

A skinny man with black horn-rimmed glasses sat at a computer console at the rear of the limo. He had long, thinning hair, tied into what looked more like a stringy rat's tail than a ponytail. His white T-shirt had turned a distinct shade of yellow around the collar and under his armpits. Empty Red Bull cans and candy bar wrappers littered his workstation. "What were all those alarms going off for?" he asked.

"That is what we need to determine, Mr. Kowalski," Caine answered.

Harold Kowalski was a twenty-five-year-old genius Caine had recruited straight from MIT after letting his previous computer analyst go—from a twentieth-story window—for failing to meet expectations. Kowalski had almost been arrested for hacking into the Pentagon's Homeland Security when Caine intervened. He paid off the appropriate officials and absorbed the university student into his enterprise. Kowalski's performance had been impeccable—until today.

Mussels passed the surveillance SD card to the computer analyst. Kowalski pushed it into a slot and started punching keys. An image of the exhibit's darkened interior popped onto the screen. No movement could be detected. He pressed the fast-forward button. A girl suddenly appeared in the middle of the room.

Kowalski skipped backward and let the events unfold in real time. As if stepping out from some invisible bubble, the girl materialized on the screen again. "That must be the witch," he announced. "She's young. I thought witches couldn't teleport from one place to the next."

"They can't," Caine said, dropping exactly three ice cubes into a glass tumbler and poured himself a drink from the bar. He watched the girl move from one display case to the next before stopping in front of the runestone.

He swirled the cubes in his drink. They clinked against the crystal.

Kids. They're recruiting kids now.

He sipped the clear, brown liquid, savoring its sweet taste.

Sending kids meant the Coven's company of witches was dwindling. The Inquisition was gaining the upper hand in the war.

The war would have been over a long time ago if the Inner Circle had listened to me. The Inner Circle represented the Inquisition's leadership, a small group of powerful men and women from around the world. Caine cursed them for not showing more resolve, unwilling to do what was necessary in order to achieve total victory.

He focused on the young witch again. There was something familiar about her. Was it her face, her long black hair, the way she moved?

"Find out who she is," he ordered.

Kowalski swept the computer's cursor from one icon to the next, clicking the mouse several times. A three-dimensional grid superimposed over the girl's face, scanning, and downloading her features.

"Checking school directories for a match."

The girl's image moved to the upper-left corner as the computer infiltrated the school district database. Pictures of teenage girls flashed by at a rate of one thousand pics per minute. They only needed five seconds.

"We have a hit. Sarah Finn—enrolled at Bayview Secondary three weeks ago."

Caine's posture perked up.

Finn. The daughter of Rachel Finn? No wonder she looks familiar.

"She lives with an uncle, Alfred Grigsby," Kowalski continued. "He seems to be her legal guardian. They live on 4545 Puhallo Drive."

"She wouldn't be stupid enough to go home—if that even is her real address," Caine said. "But we can still find her. Monitor all mobile phone activity in the Vancouver area. Match conversations to key words: museum, Sarah Finn, Alfred Grigsby, Grayle Rowen, Bayview. If she has a cell phone, which I wager she does, we should be able to pinpoint her location."

The girl continued to appear and disappear at random on the computer screen. Startled by something in the room, she suddenly hid behind a display case.

"Who is that, chef?" Mussels pointed to a woman dressed in flowing black robes entering the frame. The camera was unable to capture her face.

Caine leaned forward. "Apparently, our trap lured more than one magical being," he said.

"It's a deity, sir. A goddess," Kowalski confirmed, cross-referencing the figure with the Inquisition's SCD—Supernatural Creatures Database. "She appears to be of Norse origin."

They watched as the young witch revealed herself from behind her hiding place. Then, as though knocked over by some unseen force, she skidded along the floor, narrowly missing an energy blast shot from the goddess's hands.

What is going on here?

"I think there might be a third person in the room," Mussels offered.

"I pay you to protect, not to think," Caine growled, his frustration beginning to boil over. He took a deep breath and forced himself to calm down.

He watched the black-robed figure hurl another bolt of lightning at what seemed like nothing at all. For a fraction of a second, Caine thought he saw the image of a boy appear and disappear as the magical discharge found its target. The recording jolted. The scene inside the museum exhibit suddenly replaced by white noise and static. Whatever magical force the deity flashed from her hands had ricocheted and taken out their hidden camera.

"Mr. Kowalski, you were in charge of analyzing every possible contingency for this operation," Caine said, turning to the programmer. "Tell me, how is it that a witch *and* a goddess were able to escape your trap?"

"I don't know." The young man seemed unaware of how much his life depended on his next few words. "I programmed the museum's failsafes to momentarily switch off. No one in the security office would have noticed. Their instruments were set to show everything working properly, their cameras switched to playing a loop."

"I see." Caine cleared his throat. "Who is your assistant, Mr. Kowalski?"

"David Strauss."

"Is he back at headquarters?"

"He should be."

"Good." Caine flipped the intercom switch to the limo driver one more time. "Notify David Strauss to do a complete search for a Grayle Rowen in our database. I want to know everything about this boy by the time we reach Caine Tower."

"Yes, sir" the driver replied over the static-free connection.

"But I can do that from here," Kowalski said. "David's an amateur compared to me."

The billionaire produced a half smile. "That may be the case, Mr. Kowalski, but for the next few minutes you will be busy learning the company's policy for failure." He snapped his fingers.

Mussels grabbed Kowalski around the neck, forcing him down in his seat.

"Leave his face and fingers intact," Caine said.

Kowalski's eyes went wide as plates. "No, you can't be serious." He squirmed in the bodyguard's grip. "It was an unforeseeable variant within the parameters. If you hadn't put so much iron in the exhibit, scrambling my signals, I could've—"

"And don't get any blood on the upholstery," Caine added, sitting back and emptying the last of his drink.

Chapter 8

William Snodgrass distanced himself from the teenagers around him. He had to get away for three reasons.

One, he hated teenagers.

Two, he had to contact his employer.

And three, he *really* hated teenagers.

He made for the museum exit, weaving past the throng of cameramen, photographers, and reporters still interviewing guests. He was almost out the doors when Britney Astor cut him off.

"Mr. Snodgrass, where are you going? You're not leaving without us, are you?"

He was no longer William Snodgrass. He never really was. The name had served as a means to an end—a disguise, one more alias among hundreds he'd used. He put his palm on the girl's face and pushed her out of way, deriving some pleasure from invading her space and the inappropriateness of the act.

The girl gasped, slapping his hand away indignantly. "How dare you!" she called after him. "My father will hear about this! You'll be fired! You hear me? You won't work in this city again!"

He ignored her empty threats and continued out the museum doors.

Once out of sight, Snodgrass pulled off his wig and fake nose. The prosthetic glue snapped as he peeled away his two fake ears. Ragged scars bulged where his ears should have been. They'd been cut off years earlier by Somali pirates trying to torture classified information out of him. He never divulged the intel and, after his eventual rescue, made the pirates pay dearly—cutting off each of *their* ears in turn and hanging them like medals around their necks.

The gruesome act had become his trademark.

He rubbed the fleshy tissue.

He'd become a ghost of his former self since the mutilation. After leaving the Marine Corps, he'd transformed himself into an operative, assassin, mercenary, witch hunter, and a list of other titles that suited his employer's needs.

His employer. The Inquisition.

They need an update.

He pulled out his cell phone and tapped a series of numbers linking him directly to his superiors. The carrier wave would bounce from cell tower to cell tower, making their conversation both confidential and untraceable.

"Report," a man answered.

Sometimes the voice on the other line belonged to an Asian woman, other times a stuttering old man. This voice, however, was new. *Middle-aged*, Snodgrass guessed. *With a slight Irish accent.*

"The two assets breached the exhibit and escaped Caine's trap," he said.

"With the runestone?" the man asked.

"Negative. I don't have all the intel yet, but an altercation took place inside the exhibit. Someone else has acquired the artifact."

"Caine?"

"I don't believe so, sir. He seemed agitated although he was doing his best to hide it."

"It appears we have a third player in the game, then. Did the boy and girl escape together?"

"Affirmative. I've alerted the authorities that they're missing. If the police find them first, I'll be there to intercept."

"Very well… at least they're together, just as we'd hoped. And if Caine doesn't have the runestone, we can still proceed as planned."

"Then this part of my mission is over?" Snodgrass asked hopefully.

"Correct."

He exhaled. The assignment had been a frustrating one. Impersonating a substitute teacher, putting up with these punks, and not being able to kill a single one had been difficult. He would rather infiltrate a Colombian drug lord's compound single-handedly than relive these last two weeks again.

"What are my new orders, sir?"

"Keep surveillance on Caine. He will not give up his pursuit of the runestone or witch so easily."

At that moment, Caine's Hummer limousine veered away. The Operative caught sight of the driver in the front seat. He wore a dark suit and black chauffeur's hat.

The Operative smiled. He had a similar costume in his collection.

"Understood, sir."

Chapter 9

The sun dipped below the horizon, washing the surrounding Coast Mountains in hues of pink and orange. A soft rain had fallen earlier, leaving the pavement glistening and slippery. Grayle rubbed his bare arms, trying to stay warm.

After escaping through the emergency exit, he and Sarah had managed to disappear unnoticed into a small, wooded area bordering the museum. They kept out of sight as fire trucks and emergency vehicles whizzed by. It wasn't until they were out of breath and the museum's alarms were distant echoes that they finally stopped running.

The new stillness and stretching shadows filled Grayle with a sense of dread. He expected Hel to jump out from behind a parked car or trimmed hedge at any moment, curling her silver gauntlets around his throat, her neon-green eyes pooling over him like toxic sludge as she slowly choked the life out of him. On the bright side, he'd finally gotten rid of Zito.

Grayle smiled, thinking of his foster parent in police custody, cursing his name, ready to rat him out the first chance he got.

But the police have him and no trace of me.

He rubbed his arms again, only then realizing what was missing. He threw his head skyward. He'd left his jacket in the exhibit.

How could I have been so stupid?

No doubt the police had it in their possession, placing him at the scene of the crime. Even though he didn't actually steal the runestone, the jacket and his criminal record made him a viable suspect, if not suspect number one if the police believed Zito's story. He knew it was only a matter of time before they started searching for him.

And what are they going to do if they find me? Send me back to Gloomshroud? He shuddered. *There's no way I'm going back there.*

Gloomshroud Camp for Delinquent Youth turned out to be more of a training facility than a rehabilitation center. Grayle and about a hundred other "campers" were put through gruelling obstacle courses, survival training, and exercises that practiced the criminal skills that had landed them in the camp in the first place. Like him, the others in the camp had their own unique skills. Grayle had witnessed kids communicating with animals, foretelling the future, and displaying amazing physical abilities. He hadn't seen weird stuff like that since—

Well… not until tonight.

He slowed his pace and glanced at Sarah limping beside him. Her bag bounced rhythmically off her hips, the circular outline of the shield barely noticeable. It had been four times that size before she did *something* to it—something Grayle couldn't explain.

"You okay?" he asked. They hadn't said a word since leaving the museum.

"Yeah," she said, pressing the growing lump on her forehead.

"How are you able to do the things you do?" he asked, unable to keep the question to himself any longer. She must have known he was going to ask at some point.

"I have certain… gifts," she said slowly.

"Gifts! Yeah, right. Are you some kind of witch or something?"

"Or something?" Sarah spun around, her hands on her hips. "You think I'm some sort of freak?" she snapped.

"N-no. It's just weird—"

Her eyes narrowed at the word *weird*.

"I mean…" He didn't know what he meant or how to describe it. "Look, what would *you* say if someone you just met started moving shields with her thoughts and then made it shrink right in front of your eyes?"

They stood there a moment, glaring at each other.

"We don't move things with our thoughts." The look on Sarah's face softened slightly. "That's telekinesis. We use magic."

"We? You mean there are more of you?"

They started walking again.

"I'm not ready to tell you what I am just yet," she said, "but I will as soon as we find a safe place to figure out what to do next."

"No way. You owe me an explanation," Grayle said, refusing to drop the subject so easily. "You knew I was going to break into the Viking exhibit. You followed me on purpose. Why?"

"It's complicated."

"Complicated!" Grayle said, his voice rising. "What's so complicated about telling me the truth?"

Sarah kept her eyes on the sidewalk. "I didn't know for sure you were breaking into the exhibit… that was a coincidence.

But I knew only your skills could get me in and out of the exhibit safely."

"My skills?" He tried to process what she was saying. "Trust me, you don't know *anything* about my skills."

She pressed her lips together and slowed her steps. "I know you can't be seen by cameras—"

"How—"

"And that you've been trained to break in and out of places professionals can't even get into."

Grayle was stunned. For years, he'd tried to hide his past, the past he could remember, anyway. He'd known rumors of his crimes would leak out eventually, but he'd been careful not to expose the other weird things about himself. Not being able to appear on digital images was one of them. He'd never been able to explain it, and it hadn't been easy to keep secret. As it turned out, being a social reject became convenient—no one wanted to take his picture—and every year, when school photos came around, he'd skip class or blame his foster parents for not having the money to afford them. Most teachers were sympathetic and left it at that while others were too scared to mess with The Kid from Juvie. Grayle preferred it that way—staying out of people's business and, in return, expecting others to stay out of his.

His face grew hot, and his mouth went dry. "Since you seem to know so much about me, why didn't you just ask for my help?"

Sarah snapped her fingers. "Oh yeah, I forgot how nice you are," she said, not even trying to hide her sarcasm. "I'm sure that's what Britney was thinking when you stole her cat."

How did she know about that?

"And Carrigan must have been thinking what a sweetheart *you* were while she was barfing her guts out," Grayle shot back, recalling Sarah's graphic Blood Eagle description.

"I only did that so we'd get Snodgrass off your back."

"So you had all this planned out?" His voice grew louder. "This was all some elaborate scheme so you could get your way?"

"Oh, please. Don't start acting like Mr. Innocent. You were in the museum to steal something, too. What was it… a gold bracelet? A crown?"

"None of your business. Difference is I would've made it out of there before all hell broke loose if it weren't for you."

"Hey, I didn't force you to stay."

"No? I seem to remember you *grabbing* me and keeping me there. Thanks to you, I've got the cops on my back again."

Sarah glowered. "Whatever. You could have left at any time."

"Well I'm leaving now, *freak*. What do you think about that?" He turned and stormed away.

"But… you can't!"

"Watch me!"

Grayle expected her to abracadabra him into a frog or something, but all she did was yell back, "Well, that's great… just great!"

Chapter 10

Stars dotted the night sky before Grayle's anger subsided. Apart from Sarah knowing his secrets, he was upset about her pretending to be his friend, just when he thought they were making a connection. Truth was he liked her more than he wanted to admit and was disappointed the feeling wasn't mutual.

And on top of everything else, his failure to steal the runestone meant he wouldn't get the details about where he came from. He doubted Zito or his mysterious employer had the information to begin with.

Guess I'll never find out now.

He darted across another empty street, careful to keep his distance from lampposts and busy traffic. His foster home was tucked in the far corner of Shaughnessy, one of Vancouver's more affluent neighborhoods. Sprawling mansions dotted the community, set back far enough in their lots to maintain distance from the rabble allowed to share the same zip code. Many had walls or wrought-iron gates to keep prying eyes from peering in.

Of the homes lining his street, the Zito household was the shabbiest. It might have been pretty once, with a wrap-around deck and enough yard space for a nice garden. But neglect had left the lawn overgrown with weeds, the exterior paint chipped, and the roof shingles rotten. It was as if one day the Zitos had decided to give up caring for the place.

Then again, in the months he'd known them, Grayle found the Zitos could hardly take care of themselves. Sly spent hours sitting in front of the TV, drinking beer. While Irma, his wife, clipped supermarket coupons and chain-smoked cigarettes. She did the cooking but ate most of what she made herself, which suited Grayle just fine. Most of her meals were inedible, bargain or not.

Reaching his street, Grayle scanned the cars parked along the curb. An unmarked police cruiser waited across from the Zito house, lights out and engine off. Two officers sat inside, sipping coffee.

Retreating into the shadows, Grayle hopped fences and sneaked across several alleyways. Satisfied more cops weren't staking out the rear of the house, he jumped over the low, rickety fence into the Zitos's backyard.

He padded onto the back porch, opened the screen door, and slipped into the kitchen. Lights glowed from the living room. He was about to call out but thought against it. It was pointless trying to explain to Mrs. Zito what had happened. She'd sooner turn him in than listen to anything he had to say, especially now that she probably knew her husband was in police custody.

Grayle tiptoed upstairs, down the hall, and into his room. He didn't dare turn on the lights in case the cops outside noticed his presence. He let his eyes adjust to the small, dark room. A disaster zone… as usual. Unmade sheets were thrown aside on a single bed tucked in a corner. A nightstand stood next to it, piled high with books: *The Wilderness Survival Handbook,* Sun Tzu's *The Art of War, The Amazing Spider-Man* #312, and a copy of *A History of the Vikings* opened to chapter three.

Even though everything appeared in place, Grayle sensed someone had been there. His dresser drawers were shut—he always left them slightly ajar, a trick he used at Gloomshroud to warn him if thieves had snooped through his things. The dirty laundry, strewn randomly across the floor, had also been moved. To anyone else, it may have looked like a mess. But Grayle had memorized the layout of each shirt and pair of pants. Someone had checked his jeans pockets and then tossed the pants aside.

Had the police been here? Irma? What were they searching for? One look and they should've realized I have nothing, least of all a hundred-pound runestone.

He moved quickly. The longer he stayed, the greater chance there was of being discovered. He slid open his lowest dresser drawer. It had a false bottom, a side project he'd secretly finished in woodshop. He lifted it, relieved to see a flashlight, matches, some oat bars, and a wad of cash—nine hundred fifty-five dollars—rolled in an elastic band. It wasn't enough to live on for long, but it would have to do.

I can always steal more, he told himself.

Grayle stuffed the money in his pocket and the other items into his backpack. He plucked a hoodie from the floor and put it on. The cotton soothed his freezing arms. Then he exited the room without a second glance.

He tiptoed downstairs. The final step creaked under his weight. Grayle cursed and ducked back into the shadows.

"Is that you?" Mrs. Zito called out in her scratchy voice. She entered the living room, grunting. The floorboards creaked under her weight as though they might give out at any moment. Her footsteps came closer.

Grayle was about to bolt when the phone rang. Irma stopped and turned to answer it.

"Hello? Oh, it's you," she snarled, her voice switching from sweet to sour in a second. "A fine mess you put us in... what happened?"

Grayle assumed it was Sly using his one free phone call.

He chanced a peek around the corner. Mrs. Zito was a blob of a woman with hair like a Brillo pad, multiple chins, and two thin lips set in a permanent scowl. Her bulbous body was decked out in a flower-print dress that looked more like a discarded window curtain.

The woman waddled back and forth, the phone clutched to her ear. "I don't know where he is. You were supposed to keep an eye on him."

She paused and placed a pudgy hand on her hip. "If it was up to me, I wouldn't have let him go in the first place, but you thought it was time he... wait, shut up, there's something on the news..."

She snatched the television remote and turned up the volume.

"Two suspects are being sought after a daring theft from the Vancouver Museum this afternoon," the news anchor reported. "While the police have one man in custody, they are still searching for two missing teenagers sought in connection with today's theft. Grayle Rowen and Sarah Finn, both fifteen, were members of a high-school field trip and last seen in the museum shortly before priceless artifacts were stolen."

Grayle's eyes widened as images of the ruined Viking exhibit panned across the television. The scene cut to a girl's face, bright lights focusing on her mascara-streaked cheeks. It was Britney Astor.

"I was like, so scared." Her bottom lip quivered. "When the alarms came on, like everyone started running for the exits, and I was like, pushed to the ground and…" Carrigan moved in and hugged her friend. "I did get Jameson Blaze's autograph, though," she sniffled.

Next, the scene cut to Alistair Thorn's beaming face. "That was awesome! All of a sudden, the alarms started going like *woop! Woop! Woop!* And then the police and guards swarmed the place."

"Do you know the two students who may have been responsible for this?" the reporter asked.

"Yeah, but they didn't do it."

"How can you be sure?"

"Hey, just 'cause a guy's got a bad rap doesn't mean he's automatically guilty. And the girl—she's way too cute to be a criminal." Alistair winked and gave the camera a million dollar smile.

The television screen switched back to the newsroom. A photograph of Sarah and a pencil sketch of him were inset next to the newscaster.

"The grade nine students from Bayview Secondary School are sought for questioning and have a history of reckless behavior. Anyone with information on the whereabouts of Rowen and Finn are asked to contact the Vancouver Police Department immediately.

"In world news, more casualties are being reported as another earthquake rocked Istanbul today. Scientists believe that—"

Mrs. Zito hit the mute button. "He's all over the news… with some girl." Her body stiffened. "She's a what? Do you know what that means?" She started pacing nervously. "This is all your fault. We were only supposed to take care of him until—" She paused, listening to Zito on the other line. "All right. I'll try to keep him here if he comes back. What if she's with him?" Irma Zito stopped pacing, and Grayle saw her lipless smile for the first time—it looked awkward, as though she'd forgotten how to do the real thing. "I can do that," she said.

Grayle had heard enough. He flitted into the darkened kitchen while her back was turned. He whipped open the screen door, dashed outside, leaped off the porch, and raced across the backyard. He vaulted over the fence and pounded down the alley's gravel road. Before rounding the corner, he glanced back to see Mrs. Zito staring after him, one hand fisted on her hip, the other still holding the phone.

Chapter 11

Caine Tower shone like a beacon of wealth along Vancouver's harbor front. At seven hundred feet and sixty stories, the skyscraper was the tallest in the city. The first forty floors were devoted to Caine's global business ventures while the penthouse was reserved for his private living quarters. But what happened on the floors in between remained a mystery even to Caine Enterprise's most senior executives. Rumors abounded of special agent training facilities and laboratories testing supernatural objects. Some employees speculated it was where Caine housed his most precious artifacts collected from all corners of the world. If they had any inkling of what truly transpired inside Caine Tower, most employees would have chosen early retirement or run for the exits. But no one left Caine Enterprises without Sebastian Caine's approval.

The elevator chimed, and the doors slid open on the fifty-ninth floor. Two guards dressed in black suits snapped to attention as

Caine emerged, followed closely by Mussels. The majority of Caine's security were hired mercenaries and ex-convicts with no ties to the outside world. Caine preferred it that way—fewer questions if one of them were to "expire."

Mussels was an exception. His notoriety as a former MMA superstar made him a well-known figure. He was known as the Belgian Brawler, one of the youngest and meanest fighters on the circuit, before killing an opponent in the octagon ended his career prematurely. After losing his sponsors, he was forced to compete in illegal underground matches. The payoff was big. So were the risks. Winning a match meant putting down your opponent—permanently. Mussels never showed remorse when killing his adversaries, the main reason Caine had hired and groomed him into an efficient enforcer. Restraint was not in his vocabulary.

As Kowalski had discovered.

One punch too many had snapped the computer analyst's neck before they arrived at Caine Tower.

Unfortunate, Caine thought, *but only a minor setback.*

They passed an artificial waterfall gurgling in the foyer. It emptied into a makeshift pond filled with Japanese koi and blossoming lily pads. Directly ahead, floor-to-ceiling double-paned windows offered a spectacular view of the city while simultaneously keeping noise out and unwanted eyes from looking in. A silvery film prevented infrared scanners and other sophisticated surveillance devices from spying on his secrets.

Turning left, Caine made his way toward the tower's nerve center. Expensive oil portraits of his ancestors kept him company along the way. Most had been financiers and trusted members of the Inquisition, helping the organization maintain its status quo with the Kingdoms of Folklore.

A painting of his father hung at the end of a long corridor. Reginald Caine had started acquiring Folkloric artifacts over fifty years ago—a decision that had inextricably changed Sebastian's life forever.

He glanced at the painting, as he did every time he passed it. He'd committed each hair and wrinkle to memory. Like his father before him, Sebastian continued to manipulate his position within the Inquisition's old order, gathering wealth and knowledge, securing himself a position of power within their ranks. But unlike his father, Sebastian Caine's quest for Folklorian artifacts was meant for goals more personal than assisting the Inquisition. Artifact by artifact, one dead witch at a time, he was getting the job done.

Rounding the far corner, he and Mussels entered a dimly lit room filled with humming computers and blinking lights. This was the brain of Caine Tower, its central hub.

A young man sat in front of eight LCD screens spanning the wall. Clean shaven with short-cropped hair, he reminded Caine more of an Abercrombie model than a computer analyst. David Strauss turned in his seat to greet his employer. His brow furrowed. "Where's Harry? I thought he was with you."

"Mr. Kowalski has taken an extended leave of absence," Caine said, knowing full well no one would find the man's beaten body in the murky depths of Burrard Inlet. "You've been promoted in his absence. Congratulations."

A flash of uneasy understanding crossed the young man's face.

Caine faced the mosaic of flat screens. "Now, to more urgent matters than staffing issues. Show me what you've found."

"Y-yes, sir." Strauss swivelled his chair and concentrated on his instruments. "I had to dig deep in order to find all possible information on Grayle Rowen. For a fifteen year old, he's already had a colorful past. The first traces of his existence started five years ago—no birth certificate, parents, or indication that he had a life before then."

"Go on," Caine pressed impatiently.

The computer analyst cleared his throat. "A year after arriving at his first foster home, Rowen was convicted of robbing the First Dominion Bank. He was also believed to be responsible for a string of high-profile thefts in the months leading up to his arrest."

A boy trained to break into secure facilities? Perhaps Kowalski wasn't entirely responsible for today's failures after all.

Oops.

"What happened to the boy then?"

"Apart from being able to go to school, Rowen was sentenced to a year's house arrest. But the kid couldn't seem to catch a break. There were allegations of abuse at the hands of his second foster parent. Apparently, she had him locked up and chained in the basement every night—but all evidence to support his claim was destroyed when he set fire to the house in a botched escape attempt." The photograph of a burnt-out building filled the main screen. "Rowen was found guilty of arson and was placed in the Gloomshroud Camp for Delinquent Youth. Gloomshroud has a reputation for breaking the will of its campers after a month or two—Rowen was there for a year and a half."

The computer analyst shrugged. "In any case, the kid was released from Gloomshroud in early September and was placed in the care of Sylvester and Irma Zito—his third foster family. He began attending Bayview Secondary that same month. Although there's been a spike in burglaries and thefts since Rowen's return to Vancouver, he's managed to evade the authorities and avoid trouble at school."

"No photo of him?" Caine asked, stroking his goatee.

Strauss typed in more commands. "No images in any database," he concluded.

Caine stared at the information arrayed on each screen, considering everything he'd heard. "Very well, I want you to search for a connection between Folklore and people surviving magical attacks." Then he turned to Mussels. "Monitor all traffic leaving the city: aircraft, trains, buses. They'll try to leave the—"

"Wait!" Strauss interrupted. Two red blips appeared on the center monitor. "Sir, I'm detecting two high levels of magical energy in the Shaughnessy area. The surges lasted for only a few seconds but were very powerful."

Caine focused on the flashing dots. "What caused the surges?"

"Unknown."

"Not the answer I'm looking for, Mr. Strauss. Can you tie into local surveillance cameras to get a better look?"

The computer analyst's fingers moved over the keyboard. A street grid of Vancouver superimposed on the screen. "Negative. They're operating on a separate—" Another blip suddenly flashed several blocks away from the first two. "We have a hit, sir. Sarah Finn is using her cell phone. She's also in Shaughnessy—near Bayview Secondary."

Caine watched the new blip move across the screen. "Did she cause the other magical surges?"

"No, sir. They're too far apart."

"A coincidence?" Mussels asked.

"Unlikely," Caine replied. "Go to Bayview Secondary. Capture the witch and boy and bring them here."

Mussels reached into his jacket pocket and removed his Herstal 5.7 semi-automatic pistol. He checked the clip, making sure it was fully loaded.

"And Mussels," Caine added, wagging a finger at the body-guard, "I require restraint on your part this time."

The Brawler grunted and left the room.

Chapter 12

"**P**ick me up when you get this. Hurry." Sarah stabbed the End button on her phone for the third time. *What's taking Grigs so long? He must've realized I made it out of the museum by now... without the runestone.*

She knew exactly what he'd say:

"You went in too late."

"Yer reckless an' stubborn."

"You should never've used the boy."

She sighed. Maybe he'd been right—but not about Grayle. Involving him was a risk, but she would never have escaped from the Viking exhibit without his help and would likely be a prisoner of Sebastian Caine right now.

The last place I'd want to be. Then she remembered her duel with Hel. *Okay, make that the second-to-last place.*

She had never confronted a deity before, let alone fought one. With only a cut on her forehead and a sore ankle, Sarah considered herself lucky—very lucky. But what hurt more was losing the runestone. She recalled its aura, glowing soft and green.

Could it have been a part of Mum's runestone?

Mum's runestone.

That's what she called it—the artifact that had led indirectly to her mother's death. While the specific circumstances surrounding her murder had been labeled "classified," Sarah knew her mother had been searching for a similar Viking runestone. Only the witches in the Coven's Supreme Order knew for certain, and they were tightlipped whenever Sarah came looking for answers. But that didn't stop her from gathering clues herself.

One thing was clear—the stone in the museum had to be important, especially for the goddess of death to show up personally and steal it. And the fact Caine had been there couldn't have been a coincidence either.

Sarah made her way toward Bayview Secondary, down streets lined with oak trees and manicured lawns. Branches created a natural canopy filled with shadows and quick hiding places. After Grayle took off, she needed a place to mull things over, to think and plan her next step. The decision to go to Bayview seemed the most sensible—the last place anyone would think to look for her.

She found the school's wrought-iron gate shackled with heavy chains and a padlock. The grounds themselves were enclosed by a brick wall almost ten feet high. No one knew for certain whether they were meant to keep strangers out or students in. She climbed a nearby tree, shimmied along a thick branch extending over the wall, and jumped down. Despite her sore ankle, she landed catlike on the grass and readjusted her bag, checking to make sure the shield was still there.

Weaving past evergreen trees dotting Bayview's grounds, she made her way to the school's main campus building. She climbed the front steps, scanning the ivy snaking up the building, twisting around window frames all the way to the second and third floors. She sat on the top stair. Someone had scribbled the name Britney with a heart drawn around it on the edge of the step in black permanent marker.

Sarah knew exploiting Carrigan's weak stomach crossed the friendship-loyalty line and most likely had gotten her ejected from Britney's personal entourage. Not that it mattered. Sarah would be gone soon, even though she didn't want to leave. Attending the Outlander school had made her feel normal, like a regular teenager. More than anything, she wanted to be like the other girls. She wanted to be clueless, innocent, to worry about nothing other than what to wear or who to date. She didn't want to know the secrets sharing this world, didn't want to know there were powers out there that could destroy the world ten times over.

She felt a sudden rush of jealous rage.

She hated Britney, Carrigan and the others, hated their boring problems and their comfortable lives.

And all she wanted was to be one of them.

How would they treat me if they found out I was a witch? She remembered Grayle's last words. *Like a freak, I guess.*

Her lip twitched. Grayle was as much of a freak as she was, maybe moreso.

Sarah had asked Britney and Carrigan about him a week ago, trying to get some insight into the strange boy without an aura. They had laughed as though the mere thought of talking about him was absurd, not to mention a one-way ticket to the D-list. So Sarah had hacked into Grayle's school records, feeling a tinge of guilt as private files, court documents, and transfer notices from one foster home to the next scrolled across the screen.

She couldn't blame him for being freaked out earlier. He'd seen too much—a goddess, her using magic. Sarah shut her eyes and clenched her jaw. She'd revealed her powers in front of an Outlander—disobeying one of the Coven's most sacred rules. *Maybe I should've been more honest with him. But if he knew how different he was, things that weren't in his files...*

She heard footsteps pounding on pavement, coming her way. Sarah charged her body, feeling the magic tingle along every nerve ending. She pressed herself against the brick banister.

Grayle rounded the corner, huffing and puffing.

"What are *you* doing here?" she said, stepping from the shadows.

He jumped back, startled. "I... I had... to... to find... you," he said, trying to catch his breath.

"How'd you know I'd be here?"

"It's the only place... you and I... have in common. I took a chance."

"Wonderful. Did you come back to insult me some more? Cause you might as well leave if—"

"Look, we're in trouble," he cut in, "even more than I thought. We were on the news... and my fo-rents are involved in all this somehow."

Sarah studied him, this outcast with his dishevelled hair and those gray eyes. They were two very different people and yet so very much the same.

But could she trust him?

He did just run five blocks to find and warn me.

"Let's get out of sight," she said, feeling too exposed on the steps. "Over there, by the Bubble."

* * *

Grayle followed her to a set of picnic tables surrounding a dome containing the school's second gymnasium. Years earlier, two Bayview buildings had burned down, leaving only the floor of what was the original gym. Rather than building a new one, school officials had decided that an air-pressurized dome would be constructed over the existing gym floor. The dome was white, resembling a giant soap bubble.

Sarah chose a picnic table farthest from the parking lot. It was quiet, except for the *ch-ch-ch* of a sprinkler left on by the school's groundskeeper.

They sat, and Grayle told her what he'd overheard.

"You said your foster mum wasn't happy knowing the two of us were together?" she asked when he finished.

"It was more than just not being happy. For a second, she looked scared."

Irma Zito's facial expressions were limited to hunger, anger, and a scowl that Grayle described as her "normal" look. She'd never shown anything remotely close to fear—until tonight.

"Can I borrow your laptop?" Grayle asked, nodding toward Sarah's bag.

"Why?"

"I need to check something."

She hesitated then removed the computer and handed it to him. The screen lit up and hummed to life when he opened it.

Grayle expertly moved the cursor from icon to icon, typing with practiced speed.

"I didn't know you were good with computers," Sarah said.

His fingers danced over the keyboard. "Looks like you don't know everything about me after all." He kept his eyes on the screen, bypassing firewalls and other blocking filters. "The courts ruled I can't have access to computers or cell phones.

They were scared my abilities at infiltrating security systems would carry over to hacking and stealing in the virtual world. They were right." The insignia of the Ministry of Children and Families flashed across the screen.

"What are you doing?" Sarah asked.

"Hacking into Vancouver's foster parent database."

"Why?"

"I need to be sure."

"Sure of what?"

A list of hyperlinked names appeared under a heading titled *Foster Parents in Greater Vancouver*. Scrolling down to the Z's, Grayle scanned the listed names. His brow furrowed. "Something isn't right." He turned the laptop in her direction. "There's no Sylvester or Irma Zito in the database."

Sarah's eyes shifted uncomfortably from the computer to Grayle and back again.

"What is it?" he asked.

"It's nothing."

"Hey, if you know something, you have to tell me."

She rubbed her palms on her jeans and let out a long, drawn-out breath. "Your foster parent, Zito—or whatever his name is—he's a Folklorian."

"A what?"

"A person born in Folklore."

Grayle's eyes narrowed. "I know I'm going to regret this... but what's Folklore?"

"Folklore is where I—my kind—come from. It's a world that exists parallel to this one."

"What do you mean *parallel*?"

Sarah pursed her lips. "I'm already telling you more than I should. There are places throughout the world that Outlanders—

people like you—don't know about. You have to trust me on this."

Trust? The word wasn't in Grayle's vocabulary. But based on what he'd seen earlier, he had to believe what she was saying might be true. "How do you know he's from Folklore?" he asked.

She squirmed on the bench. "I just... do. Okay?"

Great. More mysteries.

Grayle stood and paced along the picnic table, trying to release some of his pent-up frustration. "Okay, let's say you're right: the Zitos aren't—" He cleared his throat. "From this world. Why was I placed in their care? Why the whole act?"

"I don't know," Sarah said. She sounded sincere. "Folklorians, those who live in the Outlander world anyway, are supposed to keep a low profile. They shouldn't be trying to steal artifacts—"

"Or be crappy foster parents?" Grayle added. His eyes fixed on Bayview Secondary. Despite his behaviour record and the Zitos' obvious dislike for him, they had insisted he attend this school. Why? There were others closer to where he lived, more suited for kids with his background. It didn't make any sense.

He sat back down. "So what do we do now?"

"We?" Sarah said, cocking an eyebrow, "I thought you didn't want anything to do with a *freak* like me."

Grayle scuffed at the dirt with his shoe. "Yeah, about that. I-I'm sorry. I don't think you're a freak... really."

Sarah nodded. "And I'm sorry I can't be more honest with you. I know keeping secrets isn't a great way to start a friendship."

"Friendship... is that what this is? Seems more like a partnership in crime... like Bonnie and Clyde."

"You're a geek." She nudged him playfully with her shoulder. A shadow of a smile played over her face.

He was just thinking how pretty she was when her expression grew serious again.

"Grayle, the whole episode in the museum today was a trap to capture me. No one uses iron like that anymore, especially not on doors."

"Do you think Hel had something to do with it?"

Sarah shut the laptop and returned it to her bag. "I doubt it. She's as vulnerable to iron as I am... and she definitely didn't count on me and you being there. Remember how surprised she was when her magic didn't kill you?"

Grayle recalled the shock in the goddess's eyes. "Why do you think she wanted the runestone?"

"The stone's important. It's one of—"

A sudden rustle from nearby trees distracted her.

"What was that?" Grayle asked. They sprang to their feet and stared into the darkness. Twigs and branches snapped under the weight of something heavy skulking in the brush. For a moment, the noise reminded Grayle of the creature dragging its leg through the woods in his dream. He reached for his backpack, ready to grab his flashlight.

"No, wait," Sarah said.

They listened for a few more seconds.

The stench of rotten eggs filled the air.

Grayle's heart began to race when he recognized the smell.

Brimstone.

Chapter 13

"Ugh." Sarah crinkled her nose. The reek of brimstone drifting from the woods seemed stronger than before. That could only mean one of three things: something more powerful than Hel was out there, something much bigger—or both.

"We've got to get out of here." She took the lead, hurrying back toward Bayview's main building. Grayle followed close behind.

"Don't run. It'll pick up our movements," she warned.

"Who is it? Is it Hel?"

She didn't think so. Grayle's proximity may have been distorting her senses, but the approaching aura felt different from what she'd sensed back in the museum. The new aura was something entirely different, more primal, savage.

They were about to cross where the soccer pitch met the outdoor basketball courts when Sarah heard sizzling, like bacon being cooked in a frying pan.

"Stop," she said.

They froze.

An eerie howl pierced the night. It should have been loud enough to rouse anything within a one-mile radius, but the surrounding houses remained dark. The howl was replaced by sniffing and what sounded like claws scratching on pavement.

Something was tracking them.

"This way." Sarah slinked along the school wall, keeping to the shadows. They crouched behind a row of bushes just as a dog stalked around the corner. But it was no ordinary dog. The hound was the size of a horse, with eyes blazing like headlights and a thick tuft of fur streaking down its back. The beast's paws sizzled into the concrete, leaving scorched pawprints as it walked. Steam rose from its flaring nostrils sniffing the air, searching for their scent.

Sarah placed a hand on Grayle's knee. "It's Manegarm… a Hel-hound," she whispered, not taking her eyes off the creature.

"Is this going to happen every time we meet up? Weird things trying to kill us?"

She huffed. "Welcome to my life."

The Hel-hound sniffed the ground, taking two steps in their direction. It growled a low rumbling noise from the back of its throat. Then, looking straight at them, it bared its fangs.

"Go! Run!" Sarah shouted.

"But you said—"

"Move!"

She threw Grayle out of the way as the beast pounced. With a shrieking yowl, it crashed into the school's brick wall, smashing a row of classroom windows. Sarah scrambled to her feet and barrelled after Grayle, who was already bolting down the length of the school. She heard Manegarm's padded feet closing in behind her. Pouring on speed, she felt the creature's hot breath bearing down on her. At the last moment, whether by luck or instinct, she veered left. The Hel-hound's claws lashed out, tearing her bag off her shoulder. The force sent Sarah sprawling onto the school lawn. She tumbled but shoulder-rolled back onto her feet.

Manegarm dug its claws into the ground and prowled back toward her.

There was nowhere for Sarah to run.

Where is Grayle? That slimy… He took off on me again.

"Good doggy… nice doggy," she said calmly, wishing the Hel-hound would sit or play dead.

The beast flattened its ears and growled. It slunk closer, savoring the moment before the final leap, before the sweet taste of the kill.

As Manegarm pounced, Sarah somersaulted out of the way, grabbing her pink bag from the ground. She reached inside and strapped the miniaturized shield to her forearm.

"Ga'la!" she shouted.

The shield flashed blue and tripled in size.

Manegarm took two steps back, seeming to sense its prey might not be the easy target it had anticipated. The hesitation only lasted a moment, not long enough for Sarah to form an escape plan.

Regaining its ferocity, the hound crept closer.

Sarah bumped into something solid behind her. The Hel-hound had backed her against the school wall

Seeing its prey pinned, the beast lunged and tried to force its gnashing teeth around Sarah's shield. She could smell the hound's fetid breath as she fended it off, pushing against the beast with all her might. The heat coming from the beast was unbearable. She couldn't breathe.

From out of nowhere, a stream of water splashed into Manegarm's side.

Grayle came running with a sprinkler hose flopping behind him. "Heel... stop! Bad dog."

The Hel-hound yowled. Steam hissed where the water made contact with its skin. Grayle moved closer, dousing Manegarm's face. Then the hose suddenly went limp, and the pouring water turned into a trickle.

The automated water main had shut off.

Grayle looked down the empty spout. "You've got to be kidding me."

Manegarm shook the excess water from its fur and snarled in Grayle's direction.

Sarah gritted her teeth. Grayle's attempt hadn't been in vain. Conjuring her magic, she aimed at the lone fire hydrant at the edge of the lawn.

"Vanya!"

The force of the pulse spell ripped the hydrant from its base. Water came shooting out, exploding skyward like a geyser and spraying the immediate area in thick raindrops. The blast engulfed Manegarm in a plume of hissing steam. The Hel-hound yelped, slipping in the soaked grass as it tried to claw its way out of the dampness. It cowered on its side, twitching.

"C'mon!" Grayle yelled, wiping wet bangs from his face. "This way."

"No. Wait!" Sarah called after him.

He was already racing for the school gate.

"Wait!"

Grayle slid to a stop as a second Hel-hound sprang from a growth of nearby trees.

"Manegarm has a brother..." Sarah said, catching up to him. "Skoll."

"Now you tell me."

They stood back to back, watching the second Hel-hound creep closer. Strings of saliva dribbled from its mouth like liquid magma. Muscles rippled beneath its scorched fur and leathery skin.

"Any ideas?" Grayle yelled over his shoulder.

She had none. Making it back to the hose and hydrant was out of the question—Skoll would catch them long before then. Sarah saw Manegarm pull itself from the deluge. The hound's eyes glowed hot with rage.

The two beasts circled closer, seeming to coordinate their final strike.

With no weapons and unable to run, a kind of desperate determination filled her. If she couldn't escape, she'd go down fighting. The alternative was waiting to become a Scooby Snack—not the way she envisioned her life ending.

Synchronizing their final strike, Skoll and Manegarm were about to attack when bouncing headlights and the sound of a revving engine came rushing up Bayview's entrance. A pickup truck rammed through the school's gates, sending iron bars crashing into the parking lot. The Hel-hounds dashed out of the way as the vehicle skidded to a stop. The truck's passenger door flung open. A man in a cowboy hat sat at the steering wheel, pointing a Winchester rifle straight at Sarah.

"Get down!" he shouted.

She did—just as her Caretaker fired two rounds into Skoll, then two more into Manegarm. The impacts forced both Hel-hounds to retreat.

"Get in. Pronto!"

Sarah grabbed Grayle by the arm.

"What took you?" she asked, piling Grayle into the truck's benchseat and slamming the door behind her.

"Had a hog-killin' time gettin' through traffic," Grigsby answered. He shifted into reverse and slammed on the gas.

Seeing their prey escaping, Skoll and Manegarm bounded after them.

"Here they come!" Grayle warned.

The truck lurched to one side, squealing onto the street. Manegarm crashed onto the hood before Grigsby could change gears. The metal crumpled under its weight. The beast growled and eyed the passengers inside. Drool oozed from its mouth, burning holes into the windshield.

"Drive!" Grayle yelled.

The Caretaker stepped on the accelerator, thrusting the truck forward.

"Hold on," he shouted and yanked the steering wheel wildly from left to right. With the screech of twisting metal, the Helhound tumbled, sheering off the truck's hood in the process.

Grayle and Sarah whipped around. Manegarm lay crumpled on the pavement like a heap of steaming roadkill.

Chapter 14

Horns blared and pedestrians shook their fists as the truck raced through Vancouver's double-laned avenues, ignoring traffic lights and speed limits. Steam poured from the punctured radiator where Manegarm's claws and the truck's hood had been only moments before.

"Are they coming after us?" Sarah asked.

Grayle scanned the street behind them. "I don't think so," he said, still tasting brimstone residue in his mouth. "Why were they after us?"

"Hel-hounds hunt lost souls an' track down Hel's prey," said the driver, glancing into the rearview mirror and stepping on the gas. He wore a wide-brimmed Stetson cowboy hat and a stiff leather duster that smelled of musk and rawhide.

"This is Grigsby... my Caretaker," Sarah said. "Grigs, this is—"

"I know who an' what he is." The Caretaker gunned through another red light. "Where're we droppin' him off?"

Sarah put on her seat belt. "He's coming with me."

The cowboy looked as though he were about to have a heart attack. "He can't go with you! The Coven won't take kindly to you bringin' a—"

"All of a sudden you care about what the Coven thinks? Besides, they don't need to know," she snapped.

"Takin' him'll only complicate matters. Yer lookin' to kick up a row."

"I'll handle it," Sarah said firmly.

Grigsby pressed his lips together in a scowl, not looking convinced. "Well, anyway, yer transportation's bin arranged."

"*Our* transportation," she corrected.

"And where exactly am *I* going?" Grayle cut in. He hated when people talked about him as if he wasn't there. "Where can we go to get away from those… things?"

"We have to leave the city," Sarah said.

Grayle figured as much. He knew going back to the Zitos was out of the question, and with the police and those demon hounds after them, staying in Vancouver was no longer an option.

"So tell me how things came a cropper today," Grigsby said, swerving to avoid a bus pulling out from its stop.

"He means how things went wrong today," Sarah translated. She delivered a quick update on everything that had happened since their escape from the museum. Grayle noticed she left out their argument.

"Strange that the goddess of death chose to steal the artifact at the same time you were in the exhibit," Grigsby mentioned when she finished.

"A case of being at the wrong place at the wrong time?" Grayle asked.

"More like a coincidence," Sarah added.

"From my experience, coincidences like this take a lot of plannin'. But with the goddess's involvement, I think there's more happenin' here than we realize."

"We?" Grayle blurted out. "What do you mean *we*? *We* don't realize or know anything." The truck continued to weave dangerously through traffic. Grayle fumbled to click in his seat belt. "All *I* know is I'm stuck in this truck after being attacked by…" He glanced at Sarah. "The goddess of death? Then I'm an accomplice to stealing an artifact from the museum, the police are looking for me, two freakin' Hel-hound things just attacked me, and"—he jabbed a thumb at Sarah—"she's able to do some…" He almost said *weird*. "Really incredible stuff. That's all *I* know."

Sarah turned to Grigsby. "He's already seen so much. He needs to know."

"The less he knows, the safer it'll be for all of us."

"What happens if someone else finds him? It's better he learns from us rather than, say… Caine, the Romans… or worse yet, the Inquisition."

A long silence followed.

"All right," the Caretaker grumbled. "Spin yer yarn."

Sarah took a deep breath, held the air in her lungs, then slowly exhaled. "I was sent to Vancouver three weeks ago to acquire a rare Viking artifact. Sebastian Caine was rumored to have several in his possession. As if having a bazillion dollars wasn't enough, he's been hoarding magical relics in order to make himself more fabulously powerful. Anyway, I was sent to recover one of these relics from his vault in Caine Tower. Problem is the building is too heavily guarded for me to slip into unnoticed. But we knew the Vancouver Museum would be opening soon and that Caine, along with other wealthy benefactors, would be donating artifacts from his own personal collection. All I had to do was get inside the museum. When I heard the history classes from Bayview Secondary had a special invitation to attend the grand opening, I enrolled. Once inside, I was hoping to find the artifact."

"The runestone in the Viking exhibit," Grayle said.

"That's right. But that wasn't Caine's stone. It was donated by some 'Anonymous Benefactor.' We figured Caine would display his stone intentionally for everyone to see."

"That makes no sense. Why would he *intentionally* display something so valuable out in the open?"

"Partly because of his ego—he needs to flaunt his wealth and power. The other part is—"

"We suspect Caine's bin settin' traps for witches an' warlocks," Grigsby cut in, casting a worried look at Sarah. "I reckon that's bin confirmed now. In the last year alone, two witches an' a warlock have disappeared tryin' to acquire artifacts from Caine's strongholds around the world."

"Acquire? You mean *steal*," Grayle said.

"In a manner of speakin'… yeah, steal. But Caine obtained many of 'em artifacts through murder an' bloodshed. His ruthlessness is well-known, an' his determination to use the artifacts makes him a very curly wolf. You see, bein' able to use magic is not somethin' just anyone can do. It's a gift few are born with. Sarah, for example, first used magic when she was seven."

"Six actually," she corrected.

"Since then, she's bin workin' to develop her skill. But if this power were to be used by a person not born with the gift, to be twisted an' corrupted to meet their own end, it'd have disastrous consequences."

"That's why I was about to abort the mission," Sarah said. "I knew it would be too dangerous to go into the exhibit alone, but it was also too dangerous to let a potentially powerful artifact stay in the hands of someone like Caine."

"And that's where I came in?" Grayle asked reluctantly.

"Yeah. I knew you'd be able to help me."

"But there's nothing special about me."

"You *are* special," Sarah said. "Unique, even."

He didn't believe her. There was nothing very special about *not* appearing in photographs or security footage—just a lot of blank yearbook spaces and security guards scratching their heads when money and jewels inexplicably vanished. To disappear altogether, now *that* was a gift worth having.

"Look," Sarah went on, "I'm not only a witch but an Auralex too."

Grayle shook his head. "You're losing me. What's an Auralex?"

"A person who can see the luminous radiation surrounding people and objects," she said, as if reciting from a dictionary. "I can see the life energy people and objects give off."

Grigsby nodded. "She's bin able to see people's auras since she was seven."

"Since I was six," she corrected again. "That's what I noticed about you. You're different from everyone else."

"Is that why you've been staring at me at school?" Grayle asked. "Because my aura's different?"

She shifted in her seat and nodded.

"And here I thought you were drawn to my charming personality."

She blushed and turned her gaze out the window.

"And you say I'm different from everyone else?"

Sarah nodded, facing him again. "Outlanders have a regular aura. Magically talented people give off a different glow. People from Folklore have their own kind of aura, too. That's how I knew Zito was a Folklorian. Even the shield has an aura."

"Shield? What in tarnation are you talkin' about?"

Grayle glimpsed the circular object peeking from Sarah's bag. She reached down and pulled it out.

"That there shield protected you from Hel's mojo?" Grigsby asked.

"If I didn't have it, we'd be dead right now," Sarah answered bluntly.

"Thank goodness for that. But it's remarkable that there shield survived the attack at all. A normal one would've bin destroyed if faced with such mojo, but that one"—the Caretaker pointed—"seems to have a protection spell on it."

"Maybe that's why it has an aura." She tucked it back into her bag.

"Maybe. Either way, it was a good idea to snatch it," Grigsby agreed. "It may come in handy again."

Sarah smirked at Grayle as if to say *I told you so*.

They crossed the Cambie Street Bridge over False Creek, which wasn't a creek at all but a stretch of water separating the downtown core from the rest of the city. High-rise condos and multi-million-dollar properties bordered the harbor's walkways and parks. Yachts were docked along the inlet's shoreline.

Grigsby steered into the trendy Yaletown district. They passed fancy boutiques and corporate skyscrapers. Most stores were closed for the night, but restaurants and bars remained open. As if taking a leisurely Sunday drive, the Caretaker turned down one street after another. This went on for nearly ten minutes.

"Are you lost?" Grayle asked.

Grigsby's brow furrowed. His focus darted from the street ahead to the rearview mirror. "No. I think we're bein' followed."

Chapter 15

Sarah twisted in her seat, spotting a white van keeping a discreet distance behind them.

"Is it the cops?" Grayle asked.

"They'd be driving police cruisers, genius," she pointed out.

Grigsby punched the accelerator. "Caine's men, I reckon." The truck swerved hard to the left. The rear end slid on the slick pavement. Grigsby turned the steering wheel to compensate, missing a row of parked cars by inches.

The van followed, gaining speed.

"Sarah, if you'd be so kind as to immobilize'em," Grigsby said, banking the truck to the right.

"But I've never..." she hesitated. "I mean... not against anything so big..."

The Caretaker clenched his teeth. "There's no time like the present." He jerked the steering wheel so hard both she and Grayle had to brace themselves against the dashboard.

Sarah had never used magic on anything as big as a van before. Between her confrontations with the goddess and the Helhounds, she also knew her magic was close to being tapped out.

So what am I supposed to do?

She rolled down the window and undid her seat belt. Her hair whipped about as she stuck her head and arm out of the speeding truck, facing the van tailing them. Despite the growing darkness, Sarah recognized the bulky, yellow aura of Caine's bodyguard filling the driver seat.

She pursed her lips and held out her palm as though signalling Mussels to stop. She felt the familiar surge of energy ripple through her body. The warm, tingling sensation spread from her chest and concentrated down her outstretched arm.

"Vanya."

An invisible wave pulsed from her open hand. The van's headlight smashed, and the fender crumpled. The vehicle jolted wildly, almost veering off the street.

"Do it again!" Grigsby shouted over the rushing wind.

Arms trembling, Sarah propped her torso dangerously on the open window. Another wave sprang from her palms, but Caine's bodyguard swerved to the right. The wave glanced the van's back end.

Grigsby steered into a narrow street lined with chic restaurants and nightclubs. Party revellers filled the sidewalks and outdoor patios. They stared open mouthed as the hoodless truck bounced wildly over potholes, spewing steam from its engine with a girl hanging halfway out its passenger window.

The street could fit only one vehicle at a time. If anyone came the opposite way, there would be no option but to ram into parked cars on one side or helpless pedestrians on the other. Mussels didn't seem to care one way or the other. The van's engine revved, speeding even faster, closing the gap between them.

The bodyguard lowered his driver-side window. His hand emerged holding a gun. Two bullets fired before Sarah could do anything. One missed. The other pinged into the pickup's tailgate. Screams erupted. Pedestrians scrambled for cover, dropping to the pavement and diving beneath tables. Another bullet whistled past the truck, exploding into a concrete pillar outside a patio.

Heart pounding, Sarah knew she had to do something before innocent Outlanders were killed. Chancing a pulse or fireball spell in this confined space could make matters worse, especially with so many pedestrians around.

Both vehicles shot out of the alley, crossing onto a wide avenue. The van followed close behind. It surged forward, this time ramming into their bumper. The pickup fishtailed, scraping against trees edging the street.

The van charged again.

"Hold on!" Grigs yelled.

Tires squealing, the second impact swung their truck a complete one eighty degrees. Sarah screamed as the G-force threatened to throw her headfirst onto the road. She felt Grayle snatching her legs before she tumbled out completely.

Recovering her wits, Sarah faced the van now directly in front of her. "Vanya!"

The pulse was weak and did nothing but take out their own sideview mirror. It fell off and clattered on the pavement.

"Sorry!" she called out.

Mussels revved the van's motor to a screaming pitch, shoving their truck farther down the avenue. Tires screeched. Blue smoke and the smell of burning rubber filled the air.

Sarah gritted her teeth. "Hold me, Grayle!" she said, steadying herself and aiming both hands at the van. She felt his grip tightening.

"Vanya!"

The wave dislodged both vehicles from their tangled bumpers. Still in reverse, the truck jumped a curb. It bounced wildly, sliding backward into a park bordering False Creek. The wheels dug into soft earth, kicking up wet grass and mud and leaving deep gouges in the turf. The van roared after them. Grigsby veered right, providing Sarah with the angle she needed. She forced her fear down and let her anger take over. Her remaining energy channelled to her arms, building and building until they became like lightning rods.

"VANYA!"

The spell broadsided the van, pushing it up on two wheels. Out of control, it careened over an embankment and splashed into False Creek's frigid waters.

Grigsby hit the brakes, whiplashing them to a halt. The truck's engine spat and sputtered before finally going dead.

Still sitting on the open window, Sarah laid her head on the truck's roof. Everything became eerily silent except for the sound of her thumping heartbeat and police sirens echoing in the distance. Her eyelids fluttered. The final spell had drained the last of her magical reserves.

Grigsby got out, readjusted his cowboy hat, and came around to the passenger side. "You done good, girl," he said, gently lifting Sarah from the truck window and onto her shaky legs.

"What do we do now?" Grayle asked. He exited from the driver's side and came up behind them.

Grigsby put Sarah's arm over his shoulder, supporting her as she tried to regain her balance. "Take yer plunder, youngens, an' follow me," he said, heading down the park pathway.

Chapter 16

Grayle grabbed Sarah's laptop and tucked it under his arm. The strap was ripped to shreds, courtesy of Manegarm's claws.

They abandoned the beat-up truck and hurried down a paved footpath running along the water's edge. Pedestrians stared dumbfounded, gawking first at the truck, then at the van bobbing in False Creek, then at the cowboy and teenagers fleeing the scene.

Sirens wailed in the distance. Lights flashed blue and red, speeding over the Cambie Street Bridge.

"I hope you have a plan for getting us out of here," Grayle called after the Caretaker. They weren't going to get far on foot.

Grigsby continued to brace Sarah as she staggered alongside him. "Just keep movin', kid."

The footpath curved past luxury condos to Grayle's left while city lights reflected in the dark waters to his right. Tall masts from dozens of sailboats and yachts swayed like slender metal tree trunks in the current ahead.

A marina.

They turned down a long pier, not stopping until they reached the far end. A dead end—with cops closing in…

Not good.

Grayle searched for a means of escape—a boat, canoe, rubber dinghy… anything.

He eyed the distant shore.

It's too far to swim; I'd die of hypothermia halfway across. And what about Sarah and the cowboy? He glanced behind him. The two stood there as if expecting a water taxi to pull up at any moment. "So what now?" he snapped.

Grigsby set Sarah down. "Keep yer knickers on."

"Keep my… Do you know how close we are to getting caught?"

"Our transportation's almost here," the cowboy said.

Grayle was about to protest when something large splashed in the waters beyond. He squinted, leaning over the edge of the dock. A fog patch moved steadily closer, much faster than any fog he'd seen before.

A Viking longship suddenly emerged from the misty darkness. A dragon's head rose from the prow, its toothy mouth curving into an ugly snarl. The ship glided by so close, Grayle could see the nails on each strake of its hull. The vessel was massive, at least three times larger than the longship he'd seen in the Viking exhibit. And this one was fully intact.

"Get a wiggle on," Grigsby said. A gangplank pushed across the gap separating the ship and dock. He helped Sarah up and rushed onboard.

Grayle stumbled after them.

Once on deck, he expected to see oarsmen huddled together or a fighting force of battle-hardened Vikings ready to pillage downtown Vancouver. But except for the three of them, the deck was empty.

"Welcome aboard the *Drakkar*," Grigsby announced. He snapped his fingers and the gangplank retracted. Snapping his fingers a second time, a single striped sail hoisted itself up the mast.

Despite there being no wind, the sail ballooned, flapping and snapping like a whip forcing the ship to do its bidding.

The ship lurched beneath Grayle's feet. "Where are we going?" he asked, gripping the starboard railing to steady his footing.

"Midgard."

"Where's that?"

"Norway," Sarah said, still looking exhausted.

"Norway?" Grayle knew his geography. The small Scandinavian country lay thousands of miles across the Atlantic. "It'll take us a week to get there, unless…" He noticed a blue shimmer surrounding the main sail. "Let me guess, magic… right?"

"Yer not as dumb as you look, kid," Grigsby grumbled, removing his Stetson. A plume of dust billowed as he whacked the hat against his thigh.

Grayle spotted long, pointed ears peeking from the man's blond hair.

The Caretaker fit the Stetson back in place. "Looks like we made it just in time." He gestured toward shore.

They sailed past the van, half submerged in the water. Police cruisers surrounded the nearby park. Mussels had pulled himself ashore and was being led away in handcuffs by four officers.

No one seemed to notice a sixty-foot Viking longship gliding by.

"Can't they see us?" Grayle asked.

"The *Drakkar* can camouflage its true form," Sarah explained. "They probably see a yacht or a ferry or—" She wobbled dizzily, losing her balance. Grayle caught her arm.

"Sorry… still a bit weak," she said.

"You should go down below an' get some shut-eye," Grigsby suggested.

"Good idea."

Grayle helped her to a stairway leading to what must have been the cargo hold. Before going belowdecks, he saw the dark treeline silhouette of Stanley Park pass by. A homeless man had found him there five years earlier, wandering the woods with nothing but the clothes on his back and a single memory—his name.

That was then. Now he knew about witches, goddesses, and Hel-hounds.

He couldn't ignore the sinking feeling in his gut.

Where am I going? What's going to happen to me? What other freakishly weird things am I going to discover?

He didn't have the answers, but knew one thing for sure: he didn't want to find out.

Chapter 17

The superjumbo jet levelled off from its steep climb into the stratosphere. Lights flickered, and the aircraft shook with turbulence. In any other plane, the vibrations would have been more intense, but in an Airbus 380—nothing short of a major catastrophe could bring it down. With four engines mounted on its eighty-meter wingspan, the aircraft could reach a cruising speed of nine hundred kilometres an hour and travel over fifteen thousand kilometres without refuelling. At full capacity, it could easily carry six hundred passengers, spread throughout two decks extending fully along its seventy-meter fuselage. Currently, only eighteen were on board: two pilots, five crew, security, and Caine.

Mussels emerged from the deck below and dropped into the seat opposite Caine. "We will be in Norway in ten hours."

The billionaire flapped open a newspaper, ignoring him. He hadn't said much to the bodyguard since he'd failed to capture the witch and boy. It had taken precious time to explain to the police how one of his employees managed to crash a vehicle into False Creek. Caine claimed Mussels had been in pursuit of the culprits who had stolen the museum artifacts. The explanation only brought sceptical looks and more unwanted questions, particularly about the reports of gunfire. In the end, a well-placed phone call to the mayor—and a reminder of Caine Enterprise's generous campaign contributions—cleared the matter without further incident.

Caine glanced at his watch.

10:03 p.m.

Adding the flight time and the nine-hour time difference, they would reach Oslo by 5:00 p.m., give or take a half hour.

But where to go from there?

No doubt the witch needed to return to the people who had wanted her to steal the runestone in the first place. Since it was a Viking artifact, chances were the Viking Folklore was behind the attempt. And given that a Viking goddess managed to take the stone in the end, the most logical step would be to travel to Norway, the historic lands of the Viking people. It was a calculated gamble.

But it's better than staying put and doing nothing.

A pretty flight attendant wearing a navy-blue skirt and striped shirt approached. "Would you like a refreshment, Mr. Caine?"

He folded the newspaper, tossing it onto the polished table in front of him. "The usual," he said, rubbing his eyes.

Staring out the window, he saw nothing but darkness and wondered if he was already too late. The goddess had an eight-hour head start at least, but even deities couldn't travel across the ocean. The salt content in ocean water prevented them from teleporting over long distances—a fact that gave him hope. Maybe he could catch her, regain the runestone fragment she'd taken from the museum, and decipher the clues that would lead him to the Eye of Odin.

He watched the flight attendant pour his drink from the airplane's bar. He couldn't be certain if she was the same stewardess who'd always been aboard the aircraft. It was difficult to remember the faces of his five thousand employees around the world. But he had an odd feeling he'd seen her before, and not in the work environment either, somewhere more recently.

She returned, carrying the single drink on a tray, and placed it in front of him. "There you go, Mr. Caine. Will there be anything else?"

He took the drink. Five ice cubes swirled inside.

"Yes, one more thing…"

Caine put the glass down and snatched the stewardess by the wrist. Before she could pull away, he placed the iron band of his wristwatch against her forearm. She yelped. Her skin sizzled as soon as the metal made contact.

Mussels drew his gun. "Witch!"

The woman broke free of Caine's grip. In a burst of smoke and ash, she transformed into Hel's nightmarish half-human, half-skeleton form. Before anyone could react, tendrils from the goddess's cloak whipped out like an octopus's arms, snatching the nearest security guard around the waist. The twisted fabric pulled the man into the dark folds of her cloak, enveloping him completely.

"Don't shoot!" Caine ordered.

The others looked on, guns trembling, as the helpless guard writhed and struggled. When the cloak parted, his clothes were tattered, his flesh decayed. He stood there, hunched and unmoving, looking as though he'd decomposed twenty years in a matter of seconds.

The tendrils snapped at Mussels next. But this time they couldn't latch on, deflecting off his bulk as if he were surrounded by some invisible force field.

The bodyguard never flinched, keeping his weapon trained on the goddess.

"Thor's hammer," Caine said, opening the collar of his shirt. A silver pendant in the crude likeness of an upside-down hammer hung from his neck. "After watching your altercation in the Vancouver Museum, I thought it best to protect myself and those around me."

Hel placed a gauntlet on the guard-turned-zombie's shoulder. "Not everyone," she whispered. Her voice carried through the air like an eerie echo.

"There are only so many amulets to go around," Caine said. "But I warn you, attacking any more of my men will have painful consequences. Mr. Mussels is a good shot. I would imagine even a goddess would find some displeasure at being riddled with iron bullets." Firing a gun inside the airplane was the last thing Caine wanted. If a bullet were to take out a reinforced window, the cabin could depressurize, even one as big and expensive as the superjumbo jet.

Hel stared at him, seeming to calculate the billionaire's threat. "I could force the pilots to crash the plane."

Caine smiled. "Come now," he said, growing bolder. "You did not come aboard to kill me. You're here for something… my piece of the runestone, perhaps? You know I have it." He scrutinized Hel's human half for a reaction but saw nothing. He took a drink from his glass. "Why don't you tell me what you really want?"

The shadowy figure glided closer. "You are cunning, mortal."

Mussels jerked forward, his finger on the trigger. Caine raised a hand. The bodyguard lowered his weapon but refused to holster it.

Hel's twisting cloak smoothed and fell gently around her. She moved into the cabin's fluorescent lighting. Her face faded in and out like a ghostly mist. Maggots crawled across her skull as if feeding off her death and decay.

"Before we talk business, I would appreciate if you shifted back to human form," Caine said as a centipede scurried from Hel's nose cavity into her eye socket. "It will make our conversation more… bearable."

She scowled, but her goddess figure slowly dissolved and morphed into a woman with glasses and black hair wrapped in a tight bun. Miss Jennings—the woman from the museum—only this time wearing black leather pants and a matching jacket.

"You must do a better job when impersonating my employees," Caine said. He motioned for her to sit. "I take three ice cubes in my drink, not five. All my servants know this." He wanted to ask what had happened to the stewardess she'd replaced but decided he didn't care. There were more pressing matters to discuss. "So tell me, why are you aboard my plane? You could have taken any commercial flight across the Atlantic, but you chose this one. It only stands to reason you want something from me."

"The Eye of Odin," the goddess whispered.

Caine sank back in his chair and stroked his goatee. "I don't have it… yet. And if you think I'm going to hand over my piece of the runestone, you're in for a disappointing flight—no matter how many people you try to turn into draugr." His eyes darted to the zombie standing next to her. He'd been a member of his security detail for some time. Now he was a draugr—the Viking version of a zombie. *How quickly things change.*

Hel stared at him as if debating whether to divulge something important. "The boy in the museum… he is a Hexhunter."

Caine's eyes widened. "Are you certain?"

Hel's altered face remained expressionless.

She wouldn't be here if she wasn't, Caine reasoned. "So you're here because you require the resources I can provide?" he asked.

The goddess's left eye twitched, acknowledging he was right.

Caine stood, clasped his hands behind his back, and paced the plane's broad aisle. A Hexhunter—a being so rare the name itself had become obscure, almost forgotten through the ages. If the goddess's suspicions were true, the boy could be invaluable to his plans.

"You know where he and the witch are going?" Caine asked, trying to downplay his excitement. "Of course you do," he said when she refused to answer. "Then they can't be allowed to escape. Perhaps we can come to some mutual arrangement?"

Hel smiled. An ancient evil flickered behind her morphed features.

Caine had lied, cheated, stolen, and murdered—making a deal with the devil, the Viking version or otherwise, seemed like the next inevitable step. Nothing was going to save his soul.

"Good." He sat back down, laced his fingers on his lap, and leaned forward. "So how shall we arrange the boy's capture?"

Hel's smile broadened.

They discussed a plan as dark as the night that swallowed the Airbus in the eastern sky. The plan would require precision, betrayal, and death.

Caine was pleased.

Chapter 18

Grayle thrashed beneath his bedcovers. His tortured dreams returned him to the forest, back to where the creature managed to tear itself free from the tangled branches and undergrowth. It plowed relentlessly toward him.

Grayle skidded on hands and knees in a mixture of wet leaves and frost before he found his feet. He took off, zigzagging through the brush, trying to put distance between him and whatever it was that chased him.

His limbs felt heavy. The cold, uneven ground quickly sapped his strength. Branches slapped him in the face, and roots threatened to snag his feet. He found refuge behind a giant cedar. He stood with his back to the trunk, his breath chugging from his lungs like steam from a locomotive.

A twig cracked. Branches snapped.

Grayle peeked around the tree. At first, his mind rejected what it saw. The moonlight caught a man in tattered clothing limping a few yards away. He had a rail-thin body and sunken, pale eyes. Wisps of hair clung to a decomposed skull covered by a rusted helmet. His whole appearance resembled that of a corpse who'd just risen from a coffin. A sinewy arm dangled loosely from its socket. The creature tore off the useless limb with a crunch of desiccated flesh and brittle bone. Two more decayed figures emerged from the darkness, slouching beside the first. One was missing a nose, the other his entire lower jaw. Their heads twisted horribly in Grayle's direction.

Fear and survival instincts took over. Grayle shot away like a deer, bounding through the forest without a clue where he was going.

More ragged figures appeared. They stumbled between trees and crunched over underbrush, their eyes doggedly fixed on him.

What do they want from me?

They came from all directions—five, ten, then twenty. Their gnarled hands clawed at him. Grayle turned, leaping away. Before he knew it, he'd doubled back to the lake. Trapped between its icy waters and the zombies, he could choose to freeze to death or have his brains eaten.

Isn't that what zombies do? Eat brains?

He didn't want to find out.

More creatures arrived, circling the shoreline. The rancid stench of their spoiled flesh made Grayle want to puke. He backed away, his sneakers splashing into the frigid water.

A crow cawed from somewhere high in the treetops, as if warning him to get away.

Where else can I go? I'm surrounded.

One of the black birds swooped down, looping around him in a controlled dive. A dozen more came out of nowhere a second later. They spun in front of Grayle like a tight tornado until all he could see was a blur of black shadow. As their spinning slowed, a woman stood in their place.

"Stay away from him!" she shouted, taking a protective stance between Grayle and the walking dead.

The zombies halted their advance, cocking their heads curiously at the newcomer. Their curiosity was short-lived. Staggering closer, they drew swords from sheaths tied around their shrivelled waists. The blades were blunt and rusted but still plenty intimidating.

The woman whirled her hands in a rolling motion. Standing behind her, Grayle saw a ball of white light sizzle between them, growing steadily brighter.

"Tilbake til Helheim!" she shouted.

A rainbow streaked from the glowing ball. It caught the nearest zombie in the chest. Cracks ripped throughout its body, and a kaleidoscope of colours burst from its eyes and gaping mouth. The rainbow wrapped around every other creature in the vicinity. One by one, they exploded in bursts of dust and ash until none remained.

A hush fell over the forest once more, except for Grayle's thumping heartbeat. He stumbled out of the water, his feet wet and numb.

His rescuer spun around, looking at him for the first time. She had a beautiful but serious face, made all the more solemn by her sad eyes. Auburn, braided hair fell to her shoulders. She wore a cloak made of black feathers, and a silver, circled-cross amulet dangled from her neck.

"Thank Odin I found you in time," she said in an accent Grayle couldn't place. She grabbed and turned him from side to side, inspecting his body for injuries. "We must hurry," she said, satisfied no harm had come to him. "The draugr have been sent back to Helheim, but they won't stay there for long."

"It... it tore off its arm," Grayle mumbled, still in shock.

"Draugr are already dead. Nothing can hurt them... except iron." She brushed dirt and leaves from his clothes.

"How did I get here? Who are you?"

"There's no time to explain," she said. "I'm sorry for what I must do, Grayle. For the good of all mankind, you must remain hidden until the time is right. You will be in danger all your life, but I can give you a fighting chance. The rest will be up to the gods."

She placed a palm on his forehead. "Forsvinne."

A mind-wiping flash streaked across Grayle's eyes.

He awoke drenched in sweat.

For a moment or two he was disoriented. He was lying on his back on a narrow bed in a small room, staring up at a wooden ceiling. The room gently rocked back and forth.

Then his mind clicked and it all made sense.

Sarah. The goddess. Hel-hounds. A car chase. The longship. He was inside his sleeping cabin aboard the *Drakkar*.

After coming aboard, he and Sarah had retreated into the ship's belly. To Grayle's surprise, it wasn't the dark, dingy cargo hold he'd expected. It was large and relatively clean, with multiple sleeping cabins built along the starboard and port sides.

Grayle plopped back onto his pillow, kicking the covers off. The ship gently swayed and creaked as he lay there, trying to recall as much of his nightmare as he could before the images dissolved into the murky depths of his memories.

Is that what really happened? Zombies chasing me through the woods? He couldn't be sure. Maybe his recent events with Sarah had influenced his subconscious, twisting and distorting the truth. *The woman had said I'd be in danger all my life. What did she mean? What was she doing there? Why did she save me?*

He clenched his teeth and squeezed his eyes shut. So many questions and never enough answers. He felt like screaming.

A crash from on deck startled him back to reality.

Chapter 19

Sarah closed her eyes and took a deep breath of salty ocean air. Her face was a mask of concentration. Absorbed in the gentle rise and fall of the ship, she allowed herself to relax, letting nothing but the sounds of splashing waves and her breathing inhabit her thoughts.

The wind rippled her baggy sweatpants and T-shirt. She'd had just enough time to throw them on and pull her hair into a ponytail before Grigsby summoned her on deck for magic practice.

That was two hours ago, and I'm still no closer to—

"Try harder," Grigs said, interrupting her thoughts. "One day, yer life may depend on it."

She ignored the Caretaker's words, focusing instead on an old rum bottle teetering on a table ten yards away. Sarah strained to feel the energy building in her body, spreading from her chest to her shoulders. It snaked down her arms like a warm current.

Push, push, push, she repeated to herself, silently pleading for the power that had come so much easier to her the previous night. She held out her hands, opened her eyes, and released the energy.

"Vanya."

A faint blue glow pulsed toward the bottle. It wobbled like a bowling pin then settled stubbornly back into place.

She slumped her shoulders.

"You need to do better," Grigsby said.

"Really?" she snapped. "Thank you, Captain Obvious."

The elf's green eyes rested on her patiently. As usual, he knew what she was thinking. Not that mind reading was an elvish skill, but having been her Caretaker for so long, he could read her emotions like a book. "You've made tremendous gains since yer mother's death, Sarah," he said. "We'll find answers about the runestone's origins. But for now, trainin' is essential. The mojo you possess is powerful an' must be channelled properly in order to accomplish yer missions."

"I know." It wasn't the first time he'd reminded her.

If only Mum had trained me before she died. Then I'd be more prepared for this kind of life.

Sarah's mother had taken her from one archaeological site to another, finding mysterious objects that glowed only to Sarah's eyes. She was no older than five at the time. Not until later did she discover her mother had been sent by the Coven to retrieve magical artifacts for the kingdoms in Folklore, just as Sarah was doing now. Whether they knew then that Rachel Finn had a young witch and Auralex for a daughter, Sarah couldn't be sure. Honestly, if her mother hadn't been a witch working for the Coven, Sarah doubted she'd have chosen this life, despite her gifts.

"Need I remind you of how important yer missions'll be?" the elf asked, jarring Sarah from her memories.

She stood there a moment, wiping a tear from her cheek. "No."

"The Coven's countin' on you, especially now that there're so few of you left."

"I know."

"There'll be challenges ahead, ones that'll test yer skills to the utmost."

She wished she didn't have to face these challenges, especially on her own. Sure, she had Grigs, but the actual work was hers alone. So were the consequences. No parents. No friends. No future—except for stealing artifacts and returning them to Folklore.

At times her gifts felt like a curse. Yet it was those same gifts, like her ability to see auras, that made her so successful as a witch-for-hire. Auras connected to magical artifacts worked like beacons that drew her to their location. The gifts also tied her to this life. It wasn't the life Sarah had envisioned for herself. So many times, she'd wanted to leave—escape from the pressures and responsibilities. But she couldn't ignore the hard truth: she was a witch, the daughter of Rachel Finn. No amount of running or wishing it wasn't true was going to change that.

"I'll try again." She sighed and turned back to the bottle. It stood there, taunting her, a symbol of her failures and a reminder of what she'd had to sacrifice. Rather than self-pity, anger began to well up inside. She thought about her mother and having to leave Bayview. She thought about Alistair, the smell of his cologne, the curve of his grin, and the deep brown of his eyes. Then she thought about Caine. She could feel the anger fuelling her magic. It raged like a storm throughout her body, even to the tips of her fingers.

"Vanya!"

A powerful pulse jettisoned from her hands, shattering the bottle and sending the table it rested on hurtling against the ship's railing. It splintered into a thousand toothpicks before flipping overboard and splashing into the North Sea.

Sarah laughed. Residual magic crackled between her fingers.

"Good," Grigsby praised. "Now you gotta harness that power. Hone it. Repeat it. Practice it a hundred times."

Sarah nodded with renewed enthusiasm.

The celebration was cut short when the magical breeze pushing the *Drakkar*'s sails eased, slowing the vessel. Cliffs topped with emerald-green forests came into view.

Grigsby looked from the cliffs to the sun, already high in the sky. "That's enough for today." He moved to the ship's stern. "We're almost there. You should go wake the boy."

Sarah nodded and went to climb into the hold. She sensed Grayle's familiar void already coming up the stairs. She didn't need her ability to read auras to see he was shaken from some ordeal. A nightmare, maybe?

Or coming to grips with what I'd exposed him to?

"Did you sleep well?" she asked, ignoring the perpetual emptiness that surrounded him.

"No, not with all the racket up here. What the heck's going on?"

"Magic practice."

His eyes drifted to what was left of the wooden table. "Must have been some practice."

Sarah smiled. Considering what he'd gone through yesterday, he seemed to be taking things fairly well. Any normal person might have gone mental by now. Then again, he was far from normal. An Outlander without an aura. It was wrong—unnatural—as though Grayle was some perversion of nature created by forces lingering in the dark places of the world.

She'd done her research on beings fitting his description when she first ran into him in Bayview's hallways. What she discovered both intrigued and frightened her. But despite her mixed feelings, it was possible Sarah understood Grayle better than most people, maybe because they had so much in common. No friends. No family. She knew what that felt like.

"Look alive," Grigs shouted from the rudder. "I need you at the bow, Sarah. The barrier'll creep up on us real sudden like."

Cliffs towered on either side of the *Drakkar* as they entered a fjord.

"Why does he talk and dress like a cowboy?" Grayle asked, following Sarah to the front of the ship.

"He's a fan of John Wayne and old Westerns." She leaned over the railing just below the ship's carved dragon's head. Whitecaps crested from the longship's wake. "Elves keep reinventing themselves. Before this, I heard Grigs was a fan of gangster movies. You know, like Al Capone and Bugsy Siegal… or so my mum told me anyway. He was her Caretaker too, before…"

Before she got herself killed.

Sarah cleared her throat. "I think it'd be hard to be the same person for years and years. I mean, you would too if you were as old as him."

"How old is he?" Grayle asked.

She peered over her shoulder, watching the elf lean into the rudder. "Good question. I've never been able to find out exactly." She turned around again. "Here comes the barrier."

A dense fog enveloped the ship. The air stilled, and any traces of the fjord's existence became obscured by the misty white blanket. If it weren't for the splashing waves against the hull, they could have been sailing through a cloud.

Grayle seemed unimpressed. "It's just fog. What kind of barrier is that?"

"A magical one. Any ship trespassing into these waters would find itself surrounded by this fog, its navigational instruments going haywire, unable to get a bearing, while the barrier magically transports them further down the fjord. The only way to counter the barrier's spell is with this."

She put her lips on the end of a long, curled horn attached to the ship's forward railing. Measuring almost four feet, it had once belonged to a dragon and, as such, contained magical properties. She inhaled deeply then blew into it. Birds squawked as the horn's blare reverberated across the water.

Another horn answered moments later, echoing somewhere in the distance.

The fog began to lift.

A city took shape through the haze, clinging to a mountainside at nearly impossible slopes. Longhouses ranging from single-family homes to structures large enough to house a hundred people stretched from the shoreline to where the treeline turned to grey, craggy cliffs. Walls, thirty feet high, surrounded the city and extended in an arch into the bay, protecting a harbor from high winds and crashing waves.

Grayle stared in awe. "What is this place?"

"Midgard," Sarah announced. "The center of Norse culture in Folklore."

"*Norse* culture?"

"It's the actual name of the Viking people. Vikings were only a specific group of seafaring Norsemen who went plundering."

"And this is where you live?" he asked.

"Sometimes. The Coven sends me where I'm needed, mostly to other kingdoms in Folklore, finding artifacts or doing odd jobs requiring magic."

"There are other places like this?"

She nodded. "Quite a few. The Norse civilization is one of many.

Midgard is where their traditions and way of life survive. Then there are the Roman Folklore, Greek, Egyptian, Aztec, Celtic…"

Grayle knit his eyebrows, clearly not understanding.

"Let's put it another way. You know all those civilizations you've been studying in history class?"

"Yeah."

"What would you say if I told you not all of them died out, that some remained, hidden from the rest of the world in remote areas, magically camouflaged right under your nose?"

"If I hadn't seen what I saw yesterday and what I'm seeing now, I'd say you were crazy."

Sarah imagined the next few days were about to get even crazier. She fixed the city with a hard stare and bit her lip, suddenly second-guessing her decision to bring Grayle along. What would the Vikings do if they discovered what he was?

She had taken him from the only life he'd ever known. Granted, it wasn't the best life, but there was no denying everything was about to change. Grayle would never be the same after this, and it would be her fault if things went wrong.

No.

Grayle, the runestone, and Hel's sudden appearance were linked somehow. She *had* to bring him. It was too much of a coincidence. And as Grigsby had said, *"Coincidences like this take a lot of planning."*

Chapter 20

Grayle watched the *Drakkar's* mooring lines magically tether themselves to Midgard's pier. The ropes moved like snakes, coiling around the dock's wooden posts, securing the ship in place.

Strange. This time yesterday, he was getting ready for his first field trip. Now, he was on the run with a witch and an elf, docked in a hidden city on the other side of the world.

Grigsby sat on the ship's railing, smoking from a long wooden pipe. The elf studied the palace near the mountain's summit. He dropped his gaze and glanced at Grayle, grimacing when their eyes met.

"You don't seem happy to be here," Grayle said.

"I ain't happy about a lotta things."

"Me tagging along being one of them?"

Grigsby's eyes narrowed. Smoke puffed from the corners of his mouth. "You might say that."

"It's not like I had a choice after those Hel-hounds came after us."

The elf took another long drag before answering. "You ain't any good for Sarah. Trouble finds you, kid. An' it's only goin' to get worse."

"I'm not going to do anything to hurt her," he said, figuring the Caretaker was just being overprotective.

"That's right, yer not."

Sarah re-emerged on deck before the elf could say more. She'd changed into a white flowing gown reaching down to her ankles and tied at the waist with a decorative leather belt. Runes embroidered the robe's cuffs and hemline. Her hair was tied together in one long braid.

Grayle's jaw dropped. She looked good—not that she hadn't looked good before—but now she looked even better than good. She was beautiful.

Grigsby came up and patted her on the shoulder. "Take care of yerself, you hear? Especially with *him* around." He scowled at Grayle.

She nodded and motioned for Grayle to follow.

"You know, I really think he's starting to like me," Grayle said as they plodded across the gangplank.

"Don't take it personally. Grigsby doesn't really like anyone, but he's okay once he warms up to you."

"And how long does that take?"

Sarah laughed. "About a hundred years."

"Well, it's his loss. With my charismatic personality, I'm actually quite likeable."

"The verdict is still out on that one."

"You don't think I'm likeable?"

"I haven't made up my mind yet."

"Take your time," Grayle said with a crooked grin. "Looks like I'll be sticking around for a while." He was hoping for another playful comeback, but Sarah nervously readjusted the bag on her shoulder.

They tromped down the pier.

"So why isn't Grigsby coming with us? Not that I'm complaining."

"Elves aren't welcome in Midgard," she said.

"How come?"

"Those are the rules."

"What rules?"

"Beings from other Norse realms are forbidden from entering Midgard," she explained, "and Grigs is from Alfheim, the land of elves."

"Is Helheim one of these forbidden realms?" Grayle remembered the mysterious woman mentioning the place in his dream.

Sarah threw him a sidelong look. "How do you know about Helheim?"

Grayle detected the edge in her tone. "I read about it in one of our history books." He wasn't ready to tell her about his nightmares yet.

"Yes," she answered, eyeing him suspiciously. "*No one* from there is welcome in Midgard… or any other Folklore Kingdom, for that matter."

They approached Midgard's walls. Guards dressed in leaf mail and armed with seven-foot pikes patrolled the ramparts. One guard, with a great plume of horsehair trailing from his helmet, shouted orders.

The hinges supporting the gate's massive weight groaned as the twenty-foot double doors opened just enough to let them in.

"Reminds me of *Jurassic Park*," Grayle said.

"Vikings can be as deadly as a *T. rex*," Sarah cautioned. "They have a tendency to draw their weapons first and ask questions later. So be careful what you say and how you act around here, okay?"

"I'll be quiet and inconspicuous," Grayle joked but made a mental note to keep his mouth shut.

Sarah didn't seem amused, throwing him another nervous glance.

Passing through the fortifications, Grayle felt as if he'd been transported back in time. The road ahead, if one could call it a road, was potholed and thick with mud. Pigs, chickens, and geese ran freely in the muck. People bustled up and down raised sidewalks made from split logs, joining a number of wooden longhouses that lined the main road. They traded with merchants whose stalls offered everything imaginable—spices, furs, armor, weapons, jewellery, and rolls of cloth and silk. The noises around him rose to a pitch—laughter, sellers calling out to customers, and horses' hooves clopping in the mud.

Two women, dressed in long pleated petticoats, bowed as Sarah passed. "*Velkommen, magicker*," they said before continuing on their way. The greeting happened several more times: an old woman seated in front of a loom, a boy struggling to carry two water buckets balanced on stick over his shoulders, and a blacksmith calling out from inside his workshop.

Children giggled and stared at the strange outsider wearing a scorched T-shirt and torn blue jeans. *So much for remaining inconspicuous,* Grayle thought.

"Where exactly are we going?" he asked.

Sarah pointed to the palace dominating Midgard's highest point. "The Great Hall."

Grayle eyed a staircase winding its way a thousand feet up the mountainside. "Please tell me there's an elevator—or a chairlift at least."

There was neither, but despite the staircase steadily growing steeper and at times branching off in two, even three directions, Grayle soon forgot about the climb and lost himself in the surrounding scenery. To his left, terraced fields cut into the mountain ridge where farmers tilled soil with hoes made from deer antler. To his right, a waterfall plunged down a steep gorge, spilling into a pool far below. A rainbow shimmered in the churning mist.

"This place is pretty cool," he said.

Sarah didn't seem to share his enthusiasm, somberly climbing each step as though she were heading to math class. "Midgard was originally built as a fortress to protect mankind from giants," she said.

"Giants? You're kidding."

The girl shook her head. "We share this world with dwarves, giants, elves, trolls—"

"Hel-hounds," Grayle cut in.

She nodded. "And Hel-hounds. They make up some of Folklore's Mythic Races. We leave each other alone for the most part, but there were times when old rivalries surfaced and blood was spilled. That's why beings from other realms aren't allowed in Midgard."

"How many realms are there?"

"Nine… and that's only in the Norse Folklore. Asgard, Vanaheim, Alfheim, Jotunheim, Nidavellir, Svartalheim, Muspell, Midgard, and Helheim… Hel's domain. Anyway, things got worse when a group of powerful humans began murdering witches and warlocks during the thirteenth century. They saw magic as a threat to their power and hunted us down. They called themselves the Inquisition."

Grayle thought the name sounded familiar. "Didn't the Inquisition burn witches during the Middle Ages?"

"Burned, drowned, hanged—they regarded us as pests, an infestation that needed exterminating." She clenched her jaw.

"They nearly wiped out the Mythic Races—most of Grigsby's family was killed during the Great Purge. Anyone who helped protect magickers were branded as sympathizers. We were forced to retreat into the remote corners of the world. Midgard became one of these sanctuaries. There's been a fragile truce between Folklore and the Inquisition for over a hundred years now, but witches are mysteriously disappearing again. Just a month ago, the Three Norns vanished during a trip to Egypt."

"Sorry… the Three *Norns?*"

"The Vikings' spinners of destiny, the weavers of our fates," she tried to explain. "Every Folklore Kingdom is on high alert. We think the Inquisition may be behind the abduction, but we don't have any proof."

Grayle nodded as though he understood, but he didn't. Realms, the Great Purge, Norns, Mythic Races, the Inquisition—it was too much to process. He peered down the way they'd come. From this altitude, the buildings below looked like miniature dollhouses. "How many people live here?" he asked.

"Almost five thousand."

"And they're all witches and wizards?"

"Warlocks," Sarah corrected. "Witches and warlocks. No, only a few are born with the gift… or curse, depending on how you look at it."

They stopped as an old man herded his pigs across their path. He lifted his leather cap toward Sarah then prodded the animals with a curved stick to hurry them along.

"It's becoming more and more rare to find people who can manipulate magic," Sarah said. "It's even more unique to find someone with multiple abilities like me. You might say I'm special."

"Maybe I should start bowing to you, too," Grayle said.

She flashed a grin.

The last pig squealed by, and they resumed their climb.

"With so few witches and warlocks left, teenagers have been asked to take on missions, even though many of us aren't ready. We're treated with a fair bit of respect, like royalty in some places, but you don't want to push your luck here in Midgard. Vikings have always been overly superstitious and untrusting."

They passed through a smaller set of fortified gates, finally reaching the Great Hall. The enormous structure boasted elaborate architecture with high peaks and intricate carvings of dragons, twisting serpents, deer, and wild boar. Tree trunks, larger than Grayle had ever seen, functioned as columns and crossbeams. They were adorned with golden abstract designs, gleaming brilliantly despite the dull light leaking through the cloud cover above.

Grayle figured the hall was twice the size of any shopping mall he'd seen back home. "Okay, so you didn't have a chairlift, but please tell me you've got an indoor pool or arcade in there."

Sarah never answered. She was focused on two Vikings, flanked by armored guards, waiting by the Hall's entrance. The taller of the two had braided black hair and a beard reaching down to his generous belly. He wore a bearskin draped over his shoulders. Next to him, sporting a shaven head and a white beard, was an elderly man, seventy, maybe eighty years old. He stooped like a question mark with his hands clasped in front of him. A richly embroidered green cloak hung on his withered frame.

"The tall, dark-haired man is Haakon, our Jarl, the High Lord of Midgard," Sarah whispered, "and the other is Onem, Midgard's Loremaster, our most powerful warlock. Be careful what you say around them. On second thought, don't say anything unless you're spoken to."

"You worried I'm going to embarrass you?" Grayle teased.

Sarah's expression remained serious. "I'm trying to save you from a potentially dangerous situation," she said. "If they find out how different you are… there could be trouble."

"Trouble? Then why did you bring me here if—"

She shushed him as they approached their hosts.

The tallest of them, Haakon, stepped forward. "*Velkommen*, friend Sarah. I trust your mission was a success?"

She bowed slightly. "Regrettably, it was not, my lord. I failed to retrieve the stone."

"That is unfortunate," said the old Loremaster. His eyes fixed on Sarah, hardly blinking. One eye had a severe cataract, turning it a milky white.

If either man was frustrated, he didn't show it.

"I also bring grave news which requires the High Council's ear and wisdom," Sarah said. "I request we convene an All-Thing as soon as possible."

A boy, previously hidden behind the bulk of the dark-haired Viking, pushed past the Loremaster. He also had a shaven head and freckles speckling his upturned nose and baby-fat cheeks. "It is not your place to request anything, especially upon returning from an unsuccessful mission." He turned to sneer at Grayle. "And why have you brought an Outlander to Midgard?"

Sarah tugged on Grayle's shirtsleeve, jerking him forward. "He helped me in my mission." She addressed Haakon and purposely ignored the boy. "The consequence of his involvement required he be brought to a place of safety."

The boy looked unconvinced, scowling down at them both.

"If Sarah finds it necessary to bring an Outlander to Midgard, then there must be a good reason to do so," Haakon said gently. "But what news is so pressing that even a Witch of Folklore would falter in voice and tone?"

"It is a matter best discussed in closed quarters, my lord, away from the ears of those whom it does not concern."

Haakon's eyes flitted to Grayle. "Of course." He turned to one of the guards. "Summon the remaining lords. Tell them an All-Thing is to convene two hours hence."

The guard bowed dutifully and sprinted across the courtyard.

Haakon gestured inside the Great Hall. "Come, you must be weary from travel."

Climbing the last set of steps, Grayle and Sarah followed the entourage into the palace.

Grayle had read about Viking longhouses. They were usually dark, smelly, and built for practicality—like being able to cook, sew, sleep, play, and store everything from dried fish to valuables all in one room. Often entire families, including grandparents, would live together. But, just like the hold on the Drakkar, the Great Hall couldn't be further from what he expected. Precisely placed flagstones covered the floor while the ceiling reminded him of the overturned hull of a longship. Three chandeliers made from hundreds of deer antlers hung from the rafters. Candles adorned each point, their light dancing off the polished wooden walls. The entire place looked like a hunting lodge owned by a millionaire, a blend of rustic cottage and tripped-out mansion.

"The guards will show you to your sleeping quarters," the Loremaster informed them as they reached a set of large gilded doors. "Sarah, we shall await you in my laboratory for a full briefing. After you've settled in, of course."

She bowed.

With that, Haakon, Onem, and the boy exited through the doors, leaving Grayle and Sarah to follow their escorts deeper into the Hall.

"Who's the bratty kid?" Grayle whispered. "For someone who's no older than us, he seems pretty high on himself."

"That was Lothar, the second son of Erik the Red," Sarah replied. "A warlock-in-training who may be the next ruler of Midgard, so we have to make nice."

"And what's an All-Thing?"

"A meeting of Midgard's High Council."

"And what's a—"

She scrunched her face and held a finger to her lips.

They were led up several staircases and corridors, so many Grayle lost count.

Each hallway featured doors of varying sizes. He peered through an open doorway, hoping to see a skating rink or the entrance to a movie theatre. Instead, the room was filled with floor-to-ceiling electronic equipment: computer consoles, giant flat-screen monitors, and state-of-the-art communications systems. A heavy-set Viking poked away at a keyboard with his index fingers. A double-bladed axe rested on the hard drive next to him.

Farther along, they passed a tree-lined garden containing a mixture of statues and upright stones buried among evergreen trees. Grayle caught his breath when he spied a familiar symbol carved at the top of one stone: a cross with a circle surrounding it—identical to the woman's amulet in his dream. He wanted to investigate further, but their escorts led them away.

Climbing two more staircases and weaving along several more hallways, they finally stopped at a door at the end of another long corridor. A guard opened it, and they stepped inside.

The room was extravagant, something Grayle might imagine seeing in a five-star resort, not a Viking city lost in time. A king-size bed dominated the room, complete with soft animal furs for blankets. The bathroom was larger than his whole room in Zito's house, with a tub that could easily fit four of him.

Sarah lifted an eyebrow. "What do you think?"

"Not bad," Grayle had to admit. "Not at all what I expected."

"Which was…?"

"I don't know. Something less modern, I guess."

"Don't let the pig farms and muddy roads fool you. While Folklorians maintain the traditions of their forefathers, they're not blind for the need to evolve as the world changes. That's been the secret to our survival all this time."

She slid open a drawer underneath a mounted flatscreen TV. An Xbox One console sat inside with a collection of warrior-oriented games.

"Sweet, the new *Halo*."

"And there's also the latest version of *Thief*," Sarah pointed out. "You should be good at that one."

"Ha ha," Grayle laughed sarcastically.

"Magicker, if you'll come with us," one of the guards interrupted. He bowed in Sarah's direction and exited the room.

"I'll see you in a bit." Sarah gave Grayle a look that said *stay out of trouble* before closing the door behind her.

He would have been happy to oblige, curious to see what Vikings had on TV—maybe "Wheel of Plundering" or "The Young and the Murderous." But after spending a night inside the *Drakkar's* cramped cabin and spying the circled cross only minutes earlier, he had no intention of staying cooped up.

Carefully unlatching the door, Grayle poked his head out and waited for Sarah's shadow and those of the guards to disappear down the corridor. Then he stepped into the hallway and tried to retrace his way to the garden.

Chapter 21

Oslo, Norway

The A380 taxied into a hangar specially designed to accommodate its size. The wingspan, fifteen metres longer than the next largest commercial jet, barely cleared the hangar doors. A customs officer waited at the bottom of the boarding ramp.

The aircraft door hissed open, and Sebastian Caine emerged, followed closely by Mussels.

"Welcome to Norway, Mr. Caine. I trust you had a pleasant journey?" asked the customs officer.

Caine ignored the question. He avoided idle chit-chat whenever possible. To his mind, it served no other purpose than to make others feel comfortable.

The officer cleared his throat. "Your passports, please."

Mussels produced the documents from his pocket. They were stamped and handed back without inspection—strictly a formality.

"Do you require transportation, sir?" the officer asked.

"No," Caine replied, slipping his jacket on. At that same moment, a black Mercedes limousine pulled into the hangar.

The customs officer nodded, turned on his heels, and left.

Hel came once the man was out of sight. Upon Caine's request, she had remained in her Miss Jennings form for the remainder of the flight. But as she stepped onto the hangar floor, her skin began peeling away. The flakes turned into all manner of creeping insects, dropping around her and wriggling into cracks marring the otherwise smooth concrete floor. She breathed in deeply as though shedding the disguise freed her from some gruesome cocoon. The security guard–turned–zombie slouched beside her.

They made their way toward the limousine. The chauffeur had gotten out and placed a stainless-steel suitcase on the limo's polished hood. He wore a crisply pressed black driver's uniform. It fit snugly around his broad shoulders and tall physique. Wearing leather gloves, the chauffeur opened the suitcase as they approached. "The items you requested, Mr. Caine," he said.

Inside the case, set in molded foam, was a folded crossbow.

Caine inspected ten arrow-like darts accompanying the weapon. "The dosage is nonlethal?" he asked. He wanted to be sure.

"Yes, sir. Enough to tranquilize a fifteen-year-old."

"Very good." Caine closed the suitcase and handed it to Mussels. "You have your instructions."

Unease flashed across the bodyguard's face. Caine knew it wasn't the thought of hurting children causing his discomfort but rather the prospect of joining forces with Hel. As a devout follower of Inquisition ideals, Mussels resented having to collaborate with the goddess of death. What he needed was a greater incentive.

"There will be a substantial bonus if you succeed," Caine said, sweetening the deal.

The promise of more money seemed to strengthen the bodyguard's resolve. He puffed out his chest and unclasped the hammer necklace from around his neck.

"I will await confirmation of your success here in the city," Caine said, taking the necklace. "And how do you propose to enter Midgard?" he asked Hel. "It is my understanding you are forbidden from entering the city."

"I have ways," she hissed. "You need only concern yourself with upholding your end of the bargain. Do this, and you shall have the power you have been searching for." Without another word, she wrapped the draugr and bodyguard in her cloak and vanished in a cloud of smoke.

Caine pulled out a silk handkerchief, covering his nose from the lingering stench of brimstone. He climbed into the limousine and sank into the soft upholstery.

"Destination, sir?" the driver asked through the partition separating the rear compartment from the limo's front seats.

"The Grand Hotel Rica."

"Yes, sir."

Caine pressed a button and the partition slowly whirred shut. He leaned his head back against the smooth leather seat. The last pieces of the puzzle were falling into place. Years of planning were coming down to the next few days. Caine smiled and looked at his watch. It was shortly after five o'clock in the evening. With any luck, the Hexhunter would be his prisoner soon.

✳ ✳ ✳

The Operative glanced in the rearview mirror before the partition closed. Caine seemed pleased, and for the moment, that was a good thing. It meant he was unaware of the Operative's presence or his mission.

He'd learned of the billionaire's flight to Norway soon after the museum incident. But despite having a four-hour head start, the Operative arrived a mere sixty minutes before Caine's A380 touched down. The Inquisition's Learjet was no match for the superjumbo jet's superior speed.

Upon landing, he immediately set to work finding which limousine would be meeting Caine at the airport. After that, it was a simple case of intercepting and hijacking the limo en route. Posing as a homeless man, the Operative rushed out with a dirty rag and squeegee as the limousine braked for a stop light. Agitated, the limo driver lowered his window—precisely what the Operative had wanted. Pressing a button, he released a tiny syringe at the base of the squeegee's handle. With a quick thrust into the driver's arm, the neurotoxin inside rendered him unconscious. The Operative stuffed the man's limp body in the trunk.

That's where he discovered the steel suitcase.

The intent of the crossbow and tranquilizer darts was clear: Caine meant to capture the witch or boy—or both—alive.

The Operative smiled, pleased that he'd placed a beacon inside the steel suitcase before handing it over.

He stepped on the gas and drove out of the hangar. The Mercedes' headlights cut through the dark Norwegian evening.

First, he would drop off Caine at his luxury hotel. Then he would track down the goddess and the bodyguard.

Chapter 22

"He's what?"

Sarah stood in Loremaster Onem's lab, deep in the Great Hall. The room was sweltering, filled with smoke and odd smells. Greasy black soot layered the ceiling from years of potion making. Shelves, built high along each wall, contained glass jars filled with murky contents.

"I... I think he's a Hexhunter," Sarah said. She'd rehearsed how she was going to break the news, but with the warlock and burly High-Lord glaring at her, it came blurting out instead.

"You brought a Hexhunter to Midgard!" Haakon slammed his fist on a wooden table between them, jostling a steaming cauldron. "You were hired to retrieve a runestone, a simple task considering its unimportance, and instead you returned with an Outlander— one who could destroy us all! What were you thinking?"

Sarah understood their anger. Hexhunters were supposed to be Outlanders born impervious to magic, or so the legend went.

At first they were used to track down Hexen—witches who had succumbed to using dark magic in order to kill—distorting their connection with nature and the ambient energy that gave magickers their power. Later, Hexhunters sided with the Inquisition during the Great Purge. They were responsible for the deaths of countless witches and, because of their skill and resistance to magic, proved difficult to kill.

Sarah opened her mouth to state her case but never had the chance.

"Guard!" Haakon bellowed.

The laboratory door opened, and another Viking entered.

"Go see to the boy we left earlier. Take five others and kill him."

"Yes, my lord." The guard bowed and turned to leave.

"No! You can't!" Sarah pleaded. "I told him he'd be safe here."

"Don't presume to tell us what we can and cannot do," Haakon scolded.

"Wait!" she begged. "There's more."

Onem lifted a hand, signalling the guard to stop.

"The runestone in the museum wasn't just any stone. Look." Sarah placed her cell phone next to the cauldron. "Finta." She swept her hand over the bubbling pot. Steam trailed from her fingers to the electronic gadget. The mist curled around and infiltrated the phone's components. A second later, an image of a dark stone materialized in the cauldron's vapor, its rune letters clearly visible.

"It can't be," Onem whispered, examining the image more closely.

"It is," Sarah said. "The stone lit up when Grayle got close to it, and new runes appeared. See?" She swiped her hand through the steam again, revealing the next set of pictures.

Onem stared in disbelief. "Extraordinary. Do you realize what you've found?"

"That's why I brought Grayle here."

The old warlock weighed his options. "Make sure the Outlander stays in his chamber. Post two sentries at his door at all times."

The Viking guard saluted and left.

Sarah breathed a sigh of relief.

"It was still reckless to bring the boy without consulting us first," Onem said.

"What was I supposed to do? Leave him to the mercy of Hel and her Hel-hounds?"

Haakon's eyes grew wide. "The Death Queen? She was there?"

Sarah told them of their confrontation in the museum.

The Loremaster listened intently. "You are *certain* it was her?" he asked when she'd finished.

Sarah nodded. "Hel's not hard to identify... or forget once you've seen her."

Onem glanced uneasily at Haakon. "The goddess knows," he said. "If this truly is part of *the* runestone, it was only a matter of time before she became involved. Now that the boy's existence has been revealed, she will stop at nothing to capture him."

Sarah took a step forward. "What? Why would she be going after Grayle?"

Haakon waved her off. "You will be told in time. Does the Hexhunter realize what he is and what he can do?"

She thought for a moment, recalling the information in Grayle's files and what she had witnessed. "I think he's figured out magic can't affect him, and he seems to be suffering from some kind of partial amnesia."

"Amnesia?" The Loremaster retreated, turning his back to them. He spun around a moment later, frowning. "I find it troubling that a Hexhunter has been able to avoid our detection for so long. Even if one happened to slip past our watchful eye, he wouldn't survive for long, not with the other Folklore Kingdoms hunting him as well. And yet here he is—a teenager—oblivious to who or what he is."

"Maybe it's a condition of his amnesia," Sarah said.

"Or maybe," Haakon cut in, placing both hands on the table's edge, "maybe he's had help staying hidden."

"Preposterous," Onem said. "Someone knowingly helping a Hexhunter? It would be like caring for an infant dragon, believing it can be tamed when, by all accounts, it would kill everyone around it without a second thought."

"Grayle's not like that. He's done nothing to hurt me or Grigsby."

"No doubt a temporary result of his amnesia. And what happens when he regains his memories?" Onem shook his head. "If he discovers the truth, we may be better off killing him, so he must *never* be told what he is, Sarah. Understood? Never."

She nodded.

"At least he's under our watchful eye." Haakon grumbled.

At that moment, the guard came rushing back into the room.

"My lords, the boy is gone!"

Chapter 23

Navigating through the Great Hall was harder than Grayle expected. The meandering corridors and darkened staircases wove together like a maze, with no windows to the outside to get a sense of direction.

"It's a wonder anyone finds their way in here," he muttered.

He felt silly sneaking around. He wasn't a prisoner, and he'd done nothing wrong, but somehow he sensed the Vikings wouldn't appreciate him roaming the palace freely. All he wanted was to find the runestone garden. The circled cross was the only concrete proof he had that his dreams were real. He wondered what else the inscriptions could reveal.

And what am I going to do if I find them? It's not like I can read runes.

He wandered into an area where the walls turned from wood to stone and the air grew cooler as though this part of the palace cut straight into the mountainside. Lit only by flickering torches,

Grayle kept to the shadows, hoping no one had noticed he was gone. No sooner had the thought crossed his mind when an earsplitting horn blast cut the air.

The Viking version of an alarm?

Not good.

Armor and weapons rattled in the distance. Pinpointing their origin was nearly impossible in the labyrinth. With no alcoves or hidden doorways to conceal him, Grayle chose a direction and broke out in a sprint. The more he turned and twisted, the more he knew he'd never find his way back to his room.

He rounded a corner and skidded to a halt. Vikings dashed from a chamber ahead, brandishing broadswords and axes. Luckily, they rushed down the opposite hall.

Grayle couldn't be sure the commotion was because of him, but he'd learned to trust his instincts, and they told him to stay hidden and not get caught.

Spurred on by footsteps closing in from behind, he bolted for a sliver of daylight peeking from a passage ahead. It led to an open area surrounded by multiple archways. It served as a junction, leading to different parts of the Great Hall and into courtyards and gardens. He dashed into a garden filled with trees, figuring he'd find more places to hide there than in the hallways. He dove behind the nearest tree just as a Viking shouted, "Find him! He has to be around here somewhere!"

Grayle pressed his back against the trunk so hard he thought it might topple over. He expected someone to yell, "There he is!" at any moment.

But it never came.

The sound of clattering weapons and footsteps trailed off.

He took a deep breath and scanned the garden. Half hidden among the trees were stones with runic inscriptions. Many were smoothed from centuries of erosion and covered in moss as if they'd become part of the living forest. Grayle never considered himself a lucky person, especially not in the last twenty-four hours, but as he sat there, staring at a runestone crowned with a circled cross, he could almost believe his fortunes were changing.

He crawled toward the stone, careful to keep it between him and the Vikings tramping past the open archway. Getting to his knees, he traced his fingers along the symbol's edges and studied the runes below it.

"What do they mean?" he whispered to himself.

"They retell the saga of Odin and his journey to Mimir's Well."

Startled, Grayle wheeled about to find an old man on all fours digging at the base of a small pine tree. He wore a gray robe, its fringes frayed as though he'd worn it every day of his long life. Like most Vikings, he had a beard, white and braided in several places. But unlike the others, the man seemed cleaner and better groomed.

Grayle could've sworn he hadn't been there a second ago.

"Are you lost?" the old man asked without looking up.

"No. I'm escaping."

The man put his shovel aside and examined him. The shadow of his cowl hid all but his mouth and beard. "Escaping? From what or whom are *you* escaping?" He smirked when he emphasized *you*.

"I think they found out I'm… different."

"And they don't like the fact you are different?"

"I guess not, or I wouldn't be escaping from them, would I?" Grayle snapped.

"Do not be alarmed, boy. I will not alert them," the man said and returned to his digging.

Grayle forced himself to relax. "Are you the gardener or something?"

The Viking nodded. "Something like that." He sat on his haunches, admiring the sapling he'd planted. "Do you like it?"

"The tree? Yeah… I guess. It's just a tree."

"It will grow high and strong, with roots to rival those of Yggdrasil."

"Ygg… what?"

"Yggdrasil, the world tree. You are not familiar with it?"

Grayle shook his head.

"You are new to Midgard, then."

Two crows squawked noisily in a tree above him.

"Yes, yes… I'm getting to that," he said.

"Getting to what?" Grayle asked, growing nervous again.

"Huginn and Muninn are impatient, that is all."

"Uh-huh. Are they pets of yours?"

"In a manner of speaking. They are my eyes and ears in this vast world. They bring me information."

The crows flapped their wings restlessly.

O-o-okay. "What kind of information?" Grayle asked delicately, careful not to agitate the old man. He was obviously crazy.

"Information about you actually." His lips pinched into a grin.

"Me?"

"Indeed. It seems you are a person of some importance. Why else would these people be so interested in you?"

"I don't know. Sarah just brought me here this morning."

"Sarah?"

"She's my…" Grayle wasn't sure how to describe their relationship. "She's my witch."

"You are friends with a magicker? Good. You would be wise to listen to her. Learn everything you can about this world. Perhaps with her help and," he chuckled, "a little knowledge, you would not feel so threatened."

Easy for him to say, Grayle thought. Feeling threatened had been his life for the last five years.

Grayle cleared his throat. "Can you tell me what these runes say?" he asked, gesturing back to the stone.

The gardener twisted to face the inscriptions. "Odin All-Father, the eldest of the gods, sought to drink from the Well of Wisdom," he translated. "In doing so, he would know the future. But Mimir, the Well's guardian, asked a price for this gift of knowledge—Odin's right eye."

Grayle nodded. "I've seen pictures of Odin. He always had a patch over his eye. Looks like he took the deal."

"He did. Before he drank from the well, the All-Father gave the guardian his eye. It remains with Mimir as a sign for all who come after the payment that wisdom requires."

"Pretty drastic, don't you think? Giving up an eye for knowledge?"

The old man shrugged. "Depends on how important that knowledge is."

"And what about this symbol?" Grayle traced his finger inside the circled cross again.

"That is the Odin Cross."

Grayle's pulse quickened.

Odin Cross? So the woman from his dream could have come from this place. He looked into the valley, searching for some building or landmark that could trigger his memories. The mere thought that someone here might know who he was, or at least who the woman was that saved him that night, was more than he could have wished for.

"What the runes don't tell," the gardener continued, "is that soon after Odin departed from the Well, the Eye began developing powers of its own. Legend says it can provide its owner with visions not only of the future but of the past and present as well. It can read thoughts, shape dreams, weaken and corrupt the minds of those who intend to possess it. Its influence extends beyond Folklore and into the world of Outlanders. Surely you've sensed its power by now."

"How would you know?" Grayle couldn't help thinking about his nightmare on the *Drakkar*. It had been too vivid to be an ordinary dream.

The old man removed his cowl. His long white hair fell to his shoulder and his face revealed a patch over his right eye. "Because the Eye was once mine."

"*Yours*? You're Odin?"

The old man nodded. "I am."

Grayle wasn't buying it. "Yeah, right. What's a god doing planting trees? Maybe when you're finished here, you can do the hedges around my fo-rents' yard. They could use a little—"

The old man struck the end of his staff on the ground. Lightning crackled in forking chains above them. The display of power stopped Grayle in mid-sentence.

"I have appeared before you to ask for your help," Odin said, standing to his full height, no longer the crooked form from before.

"*My* help?"

"The Midgardians will be forcing you to find the remaining runestone fragments. It is imperative you do as they want. The Eye must not fall into Hel's hands."

"Why should I help *them*?" Grayle asked. "They're after me for no reason. And why don't you get it yourself? After all, you *are* a god."

"We are forbidden to interfere in the destinies of mortals—"

"How convenient."

"And we no longer have the power we once had," Odin went on as if Grayle hadn't interrupted. "Our artifacts have become more dangerous than we could ever imagine."

"What makes you think I can or even want to find your eye? What's in it for me?"

"You said it yourself; you are different. You will find it, be drawn to it like a moth to a flame. And finding the Eye will lead you to the answers you've been seeking."

"Like what? Who my parents are?" Grayle gazed into the valley again. Could his parents be living in one of the longhouses, maybe with brothers, sisters, aunts and uncles he never knew he had? He waited to feel something—a jolt of familiarity or a sense of belonging. But there was nothing.

"You will know when the time comes," Odin said.

"When the time comes? You make it sound like I'm already going. What happens if I don't accept?"

The All-Father's expression turned grim. "Terrible things—things I won't get into now. It is important that our meeting remains a secret. The gods of Asgard do not present themselves often, let alone to mortals like you. The Midgardians won't believe you anyway." Odin stepped on the soil surrounding the sapling. "Do not lose yourself to the Eye," he warned. "The artifact will try to draw out the evil within the person possessing it, corrupting him to suit its own needs. And try not to get yourself killed either. You are more important and powerful than you realize."

Grayle stared at the Odin symbol one more time. "I find that hard to believe. I don't have any magic or skills other than breaking into places. I can't even—"

"Who are you talking to?"

Grayle jumped, turning to see a girl standing under the archway. "The gardener," he said quickly, figuring that saying "the king of your gods" would sound too weird. But when he looked back, Odin and his crows were gone. "Wha... Where did he go?"

Whoever the girl was, she remained silent and motionless. She wore layers of green and brown leather tunics. Her white-blond hair was braided tight to the sides of her head, leaving the top flowing down like a natural Mohawk.

"Who are you?" Grayle asked.

She didn't answer. The lips of her smallish mouth pressed together into a thin line. Her cold, blue eyes fixed on his as she slowly raised a hand, mumbled something that sounded like "crowker samless," and snapped her fingers. The snap resonated through the trees like a thundercrack. As the echo faded, a crow landed on the archway's roof, followed by another and another. Grayle stared as nearly thirty birds perched behind the girl, blanketing the roof in a sea of black.

At that same moment, armor clattered from the passageway beyond.

"There's the Outlander," a guard shouted.

Grayle took off running deeper into the garden. He dodged and weaved past the stones and low-hanging branches blocking his path. Despite his heavy footfalls and the sound of his pounding heart, he heard the girl shout, "Fangst!"

Flapping wingbeats drummed the air.

The next thing Grayle knew, angry beaks and talons swooped down and swarmed him like a relentless, feathered cloud. The crows scratched at his skin. Their beaks ripped into his shirt, pecking his body. Using his hands to protect his eyes,

Grayle tripped on a tree root, tumbling onto his side. He jerked and rolled to fend the crows off.

As quickly as it began, the attack was over. The swarm of slapping wings flew off. Grayle looked up in time to see two Vikings standing over him. The hilt of a sword came crashing down.

There was a flash of hot pain, the world spun.

Then darkness.

Chapter 24

A spear shaft jabbed Grayle in the back, forcing him down the corridor. Three Vikings surrounded him, prepared to use whatever means necessary to prevent him from escaping again.

Sarah marched on ahead, her posture stiff. "You couldn't stay out of trouble for even an hour?" she said without looking back. It was the first thing she'd said to him since he regained consciousness.

There was no use arguing. She was right. *Why couldn't I have waited for her?*

Sarah threw her arms in the air. "I even said, 'If they find out how different you are… there's going to be trouble.' But did you listen? No-o-o."

They turned a corner. Two wooden doors stood wide open, leading into a long, dark hall.

"Sarah, I need to—" He wanted to tell her everything, about his dreams and meeting Odin.

She waved him off. "No time. We're late as it is."

"But when I left the room, I ran into—"

"Yeah, you made me look like a fool." She spun around. "I don't know how I'm going to get us out of this."

"Us? I don't see you surrounded by these goons—ow!"

Another guard whacked him in the leg.

"You don't know anything about this world, Grayle." The way she said his name was harsh and angry. "I brought you here, so I'm responsible for what you do."

"Who asked you to bring me? You got me involved, so don't start blaming me for something *you* started. I'm not a spell you can control."

Sarah jerked away as if he'd just slapped her. She turned and stormed off into the hall.

Grabbing Grayle under each arm, the guards half carried, half dragged him into the same room. They pushed him onto a stool next to a rickety table then stepped back, keeping within a sword's length of him.

Grayle blinked, allowing his eyes to adjust to the dim light. The room was stark, looking more like the Viking halls described in his textbooks. A bonfire burned in the center with four sturdy tables arranged in a square around it. Hand-hewn wooden beams held up the ceiling. Ceremonial weapons and tapestries depicting scenes from Norse legends hung from walls, and barrels of some frothy drink rested within arm's reach of thirty Vikings already gathered inside.

At the foot of the nearest table sat a crippled Viking. His deformed legs were tied cross-legged on a shield strapped to a bench. Next to him sat a man with a banded tattoo stretching lengthwise across his face. Unlike the others, the tattooed Viking didn't have a beard and had his hair partly shaven. Both men regarded Grayle briefly before returning to their drinks and conversation.

Sarah made her way to the head table, sitting beside the blond witch who'd loosed the crows on him earlier. One of the black birds was perched on the girl's shoulder, taking food from her hand. Next to them sat the High Lord and Loremaster, flanking Lothar. The kid rested his head in one hand, dozily sipping from a silver goblet.

Haakon nudged him.

Lothar rose reluctantly to his feet, looking like a kid forced to recite a speech in English class. "Let us give gratitude to those who have answered the High Council's call," he droned with no hint of gratitude whatsoever. "We welcome Ivar the Boneless, plunderer of England; his brother, Bjorn Ironside, the scourge of Italy; and"—his voice suddenly perked up—"Erik the Red, King of Greenland." He waved his hand dismissively at the rest of the gathering and plopped back in his seat.

Loremaster Onem cleared his throat and stood. "We are here to discuss a matter of great urgency. As some of you know, we hired Sarah Finn to retrieve a lost artifact for our Kingdom."

The hall erupted in applause. Some banged drinking horns on the tabletops.

The warlock raised his hands, gesturing for silence. "But what the witch uncovered was no mere relic." With a flourish of his green cloak, Onem moved from behind the head table and approached the bonfire. His crooked shadow danced across the walls and hanging tapestries.

"Don't keep us waiting, old man," grumbled a surly, red-bearded Viking Grayle presumed was Erik the Red. From what Grayle had read in his history books, Erik was known as "the Red" not for his bushy beard but for his temper. That temper led him to kill two men in cold blood. Erik was exiled for his crime, during which he explored the open ocean and discovered Greenland.

Onem ignored his rude outburst. "We believe she's found a fragment of Mimir's Stone. We have archival records of a piece stolen from the Iraqi National Museum years ago." He swiped an arm toward the bonfire. The image of a dark stone materialized in the smoke. It resembled the one in the Vancouver Museum, clearly the bottom piece. Two lines of Norse runes could be seen and the carving of a snake biting its own tail.

"The witch sent by the Coven to retrieve it was killed during the incident," Onem added regretfully. "The Assyrian Folklore accused us of the theft, and we blamed them for Rachel Finn's murder."

Rachel Finn.

Sarah's mother?

Grayle swallowed. He never knew. Then again, he hardly knew anything about Sarah. He'd been more absorbed about his own situation, all the while giving no consideration as to what others—what Sarah—may have been going through. Sarah kept her eyes forward, trying to show no emotion. But Grayle could read the pain even if the others couldn't. It was the same look he tried to hide when looking in the mirror.

"Apparently, an Outlander named Sebastian Caine was behind the theft all along." Onem swiped his arm again. Images taken from Sarah's cell phone flickered in the smoky haze, revealing a set of shimmering runes. Grayle recognized them as the etchings from the runestone in the Vancouver Museum.

"What do the runes say? You know most of us can't read, warlock," grumbled the tattooed Viking.

"Why not, Bjorn?" someone jeered from the adjacent table. "You've only had a thousand years to learn."

The tattoo crinkled over Bjorn's nose. "I never found the time," he chortled.

The hall erupted in raucous laughter.

Only Onem's expression remained the picture of stern focus. "Very well then. I will translate."

"The All-Father's eye waits in caverns deep,
Under crescent moon it rests in sleep,
Destiny favors those who heed the call.

"The next three lines, however, are incomplete. They read:

"To stop Ragnarok…
An Auralex must…
Battling…"

The warlock paused. "The middle pieces are still missing, but the bottommost fragment says:

"From shadows blind to greed and sin,
Beware the Eye of Odin."

Mumbles swept across the room.

"What does it mean?" asked the crippled Viking.

Onem's face looked grave in the fire's glow. "A good question, Ivar. The runestone fragments, the pieces of Mimir's Stone, collectively describe clues to finding a treasure desired above all by our people… the Eye of Odin." He clasped his hands behind his back and paced around the fire. "Legend has it that Odin, our All-Father, sacrificed his eye in order to gain knowledge of the future, to foretell the coming of Ragnarok—our world's destruction. One might say the All-Father was obsessed with gaining this knowledge."

Obsessed enough to give up a body part and have crows for spies, Grayle thought.

"Halfdan the Far-Travelled went in search of the Eye over a thousand years ago, sailing to the far edges of the known world," the Loremaster continued. "It was believed he found the Eye but, understanding its danger, vowed to keep its location a secret. A runestone was created from the volcanic glass rumored to inhabit the caverns leading to the Well of Wisdom—the Eye's resting place. But fearing it would fall into enemy hands, Halfdan broke the runestone into five pieces and hid the fragments in the far reaches of our world."

Lothar sighed. "If the Eye is so dangerous, why leave markers explaining where to find it?"

"Because Halfdan knew its power would be needed some day," Onem explained.

"Needed for what?" someone called out.

"As the riddle states… to *stop* Ragnarok."

"Impossible," Erik said, mead dribbling from his beard. "For Ragnarok to begin, Loki the trickster would have to be freed from his prison."

"And what happens if he *is* freed?" Ivar countered.

"The knowledge to free him has been lost. We have nothing to fear," Bjorn said confidently.

Onem disagreed. "I'm afraid we have a *great deal* to fear. In her attempt to secure the runestone, Sarah did battle with Hel, Loki's daughter."

The mere mention of the goddess's name sparked heated curses and something Grayle never expected to see in the faces of these brawny men… fear.

"The goddess managed to take the fragment for herself," Onem added.

Louder mumbles and curses filled the hall.

Haakon stood, tugging the bearskin over his shoulders. "The presence of Hel and her theft of the stone can only mean one thing… she wants the Eye to free her father."

The Loremaster waved his hand over the fire, this time replacing the smoky rune fragment with a shadowy figure chained to a boulder. Looking closer, Grayle saw it was a man wearing extravagant armor made of leather and pieces of shining metal that could have been gold. His arms and legs were shackled with heavy chains, splayed apart as if ready to make a snow angel.

"For the time being, Loki remains bound in his underground prison," Onem said. "If the trickster god is freed, however, it is foretold that Ragnarok will begin and Loki will rise up to fight against the gods of Asgard. The gods will lose this battle, plunging our world into chaos and darkness. Anyone wishing to bring forth Ragnarok would surely try to get their hands on the Eye."

Grayle stared at the hazy image. With great effort, Loki turned to meet his gaze. His face was pale. Black hair stuck to the sweat on his forehead. Grayle could've sworn the trickster's red-rimmed eyes were staring at him.

He looked around the room. *Was anyone else seeing this?*

"Free me," Loki whispered. "Free me!"

Or hearing this?

But the others seemed oblivious to what he was experiencing.

A serpent coiled in the branches of a tree above the shackled god. It whipped out its tail, wrapping it around Loki's face, jerking it up so his eyes met the snake's syringe-like fangs. Venomous droplets pearled on each tip. Loki squirmed in his chains, his chest heaving as the droplets grew larger. Two branches inched their way toward Loki's face. The ends split as if sprouting fingers. Grayle thought they were going to poke his eyes out. They forced the god's eyelids open instead. By this point, Loki was hyperventilating. His chains rattled as he struggled against them. His hands balled into fists, and his muscles tensed.

The serpent lowered its head, slithering closer.

"Free me. Free me!" the Norse god screamed.

The venom jiggled from each fang.

"No... no-o-o!"

Then they splashed into Loki's eyes.

Grayle winced, gripping his table so hard his fingers turned white. The venom stung so badly, a part of him could almost feel the Norse god's terror and pain. Loki's shrieks muffled, and his image blurred then disappeared entirely from the smoky haze.

Grayle exhaled, realizing he'd been holding his breath. He scanned the Vikings in the hall, seeing if anyone else had been affected. No one. No one had even noticed his reaction... except for Sarah. She knit her eyebrows, watching him.

"If Hel succeeds in finding the Eye, it could mean the end of Folklore," Haakon stated gloomily.

"Not just the end of Folklore, the end of the entire world!" Bjorn added. "And what of this Sebastian Caine? Is he a member of the Inquisition?"

Sarah rose from her seat. "I wasn't able to find out. We were being pursued by Outlander authorities and Hel's hounds before we could determine his allegiance or motives."

Grayle locked eyes with Sarah, recalling their narrow escape from Skoll and Manegarm.

"It does not matter whether Caine sides with the Inquisition or not," Haakon said. "The Eye of Odin legend has undoubtedly sparked the Inquisition's interest by now."

"I will take on the quest to recover the Eye," Erik announced, unable to hide the wild-eyed greed in his face.

"Finding and taking the artifact may prove difficult," Onem said. "The Eye of Odin has grown powerful. Rumor has it not even the gods can control its power."

Bjorn threw his hands in the air. "Then what chance do *we* have?"

"It is our good fortune that there are three more runestone fragments unaccounted for. It is imperative we find and return them to Midgard for safekeeping," Haakon said. "Without the remaining pieces, the Well of Wisdom's location will remain hidden and the Eye of Odin safe from anyone who wishes to use its power."

Several Vikings nodded, sharing the High-Lord's sentiments.

"Who will go?" Lothar asked, straightening in his chair.

The Loremaster set his jaw, as if what he had to say next was unsettling and distasteful. "We will send the witches, Sarah and Brenna… and that boy." He pointed at Grayle.

Thirty pairs of eyes darted in his direction.

Me? Grayle mouthed. He felt as though he'd been put under a microscope.

There had to be some mistake. He was tempted to leap off his stool and break for the exit. As if anticipating his plan, the guards behind him took a step closer.

Ivar scrutinized the teenagers, clearly doubtful of their abilities. "You can't expect children to go and—"

"If it is not these three," Onem interrupted, "then the quest will fail."

Lothar fixed Grayle with a steely gaze. "How can you be sure? The three Norns have disappeared. They are responsible for choosing those who go on quests. Without them, it is uncertain anyone will succeed."

"These three wouldn't even know where to start," Erik added.

"There is someone who can help," Onem said. "Last we heard she resides in Baldersted, far to the north."

"Who?" Erik asked.

Haakon cleared his throat. "The Hex of Finnmark."

The room's reaction suggested this "Hex" was someone to be avoided. The name made some recoil, spit mead from their mouths, or reach for talismans hanging around their necks.

Ivar spat on the floor. "A Hex cannot be trusted."

"She's a cannibal!" warned a Viking with braids at the ends of his moustache.

Onem nodded. "Nevertheless, she may be the only one who knows where one of the fragments lies. She helped Halfdan find the Well of Wisdom a thousand years ago. She may do so again."

Bjorn stood, propping himself against his brother's shoulder. "I will not have my only daughter embark on a quest that takes her within ten leagues of a Hex, not to mention the goddess of death."

"Father!" The blond witch next to Sarah shot to her feet.

Bjorn raised his hand to stop her from arguing. "Brenna, this mission is suicide. No one can survive against such power for long."

"Agreed. The task is impossible," Ivar put in.

"Not impossible," Onem said. "We hold a key to securing the artifact. An Auralex."

Sarah straightened in her seat.

"The witch couldn't retrieve the runestone in the first place," Lothar accused. "Why send her again?"

"She's the only Auralex available on short notice," Haakon said simply.

"And what about him?" Erik said. He and those around him regarded Grayle shrewdly.

Onem focused his milky-white cataract on Grayle. "The boy is a thief, and a talented one from what I've heard. Who better to find and steal the runestone than a thief?" The logic made sense, but Grayle heard the hesitation in the Loremaster's words. The old man wasn't convinced.

"This *boy* is an Outlander," Bjorn said. "How can you be sure he can do the job?"

"We fought Hel together," Sarah spoke up. "I wouldn't have survived without his help." She turned toward Onem and Haakon. "We accept this mission—"

"*We* accept?" Grayle blurted out.

"For no extra gold but that which was promised me upon the successful retrieval of the runestone." She gave Grayle a warning glare, telling him not to make matters worse.

Bjorn shook his head. "And what if they fail? Would it not be wise to send longships north to ensure their success?"

Erik slammed his fist on the table. "Better yet, let us ransack Baldersted and *take* what we need!"

"And threaten the tenuous peace with the Inquisition?" Haakon warned. "Baldersted still shares sympathies with their Inner Circle."

"The Inquisition has already broken the peace. You yourself said this Sebastian Caine may be a member. I say we strike back—remind the Inner Circle we Norsemen are not to be trifled with."

Many around Erik banged their cups, shouting their approval.

"You were exiled once before for your rashness, Erik," Haakon reminded the red-bearded Viking. "Do not let your bloodlust and desire for power destroy all we have accomplished—"

"What have we accomplished?" Erik's bench scraped noisily as he staggered to his feet. "Too long has the Inquisition held power over us. We behave like little children frightened by an approaching storm. When did we turn into such cowering mongrels? I say *no more*! If the High Council is unwilling to act"—he stabbed a finger at the head table—"if you don't have the stomach to do what is necessary, then it is time for new leadership. We will no longer fear the Inquisition or anyone else. They will learn to fear *us*."

The Great Hall erupted into shouts and angry accusations. One after the other, the squabbling Vikings chose sides. Erik stomped from the hall, followed by his supporters. Lothar got up from his seat at the head table. He threw Grayle one last disgusted look before leaving.

Ivar repositioned himself on his shield, tucking his bound legs beneath him. "It seems as though we have no choice but to trust our fate to these three."

"You are sure this journey is necessary?" Bjorn asked.

"Father," Brenna said—the crow on her shoulder cawed and flapped its wings as she rose from her seat again. "It is our duty as magickers to protect Midgard—and the Kingdoms of Folklore—from forces that seek to destroy it. We will leave at first light tomorrow." She nodded toward Sarah, then to Haakon and Onem.

"We will meet at the bifrost to see you off," Haakon said.

Sensing the All-Thing was over, the remaining Vikings stood and exited the hall.

Grayle was led back to his sleeping quarters under heavy escort. The guards shoved him into the room and slammed the thick wooden door behind him.

His suite no longer resembled the same posh hotel room Grayle had first seen: the walls were bare, the TV was gone, the king-size bed had been replaced with a flimsy wooden cot, and a single bucket sat in the corner—his new toilet. There were only two ways out: a window shrunk to the size of a small picture frame, or the door—locked, with who-knows-how-many guards on the other side.

He plopped onto the rickety cot, listening to the rushing water and crows cawing outside. His mind was awash with questions about Loki, Sarah's mother, runestones, Ragnarok, a dude named Halfdan, the Eye of Odin, the rest of Odin, and above all…

What the heck is a Hex?

For a second, he wished he was back home with the Zitos—but only for a second.

He kicked off his shoes, letting them bounce hard off the opposite wall. He had no control over his life again. He wouldn't waste another day letting others pull his strings, tell him what to do, where to go. He refused others to have power over him any longer. Not Odin, these Vikings, the Zitos—nobody. He would go along on this mission, but it would be on *his* terms.

If what the Loremaster and Odin had said was true, that whoever found the Eye could see into the past, maybe he could finally figure out who his parents were and where he came from.

Sarah can have her gold, but I'm going to find and use the Eye before anyone else.

Someone had stolen his memories, and getting those memories back would be his priority.

The cot creaked as Grayle shifted onto his side.

He prepared for another restless night.

Chapter 25

Grayle drifted into the same sort of half sleep as he had the previous night, only this time his nightmare had changed. Dark forests and zombies gave way to equally dark caverns. Encroaching walls pressed against him on all sides like a jail cell. Yet this place didn't feel like a prison. He was underground. Even in his dream, he thought he could smell the earthy dampness. He'd never been in this place before. He was sure of it. So why was he here?

A pale light shone from somewhere ahead.

"Closer." The sound of disembodied voices startled him. They belonged to neither a single man nor woman but a chorus speaking in unison.

Grayle approached the light.

"Find me," the voices echoed softly. "Find me."

His mouth went dry. Their words had the same pleading tone as Loki's screams.

"Who are you?" Grayle asked, his words echoed through the darkness.

No reply.

The next thing he knew, he was floating over water, landing on the shores of an island in the middle of a subterranean lake.

"Find me." The voices drifted from a light source cradled in the carved palms of a massive statue. Each finger was the size of his arm while the rest of the sculpture's features were lost in shadow.

Grayle reached for the light. As his hand drew closer, the voices converged, searing into his skull like a branding iron. A wave of pain and nausea forced his eyes shut.

When he opened them again, he was slinking along a darkened corridor back inside the Great Hall. For once, he knew where he was going, smoothly rounding one corner after another, gliding up staircases and down more passageways.

They'll pay for what they've done, he told himself, not exactly sure why. *They exiled me, left me in the cold. Odin, Thor, Freya… they're all responsible.*

He arrived at a door similar to his own. Anger welled up inside him along with a sense that revenge would soon be his. He reached for the door handle. His forearms felt heavy, as if they were encased in metal.

The scene shifted. He was inside a dark room now, faintly aware of the door creaking open. Backlit by torchlight, a shadowy silhouette filled the doorframe. He recognized too late the figure's half face and glinting gauntlets. Like tendrils, the ends of Hel's cloak shot out…

Grayle jolted out of the dream, gasping. *What the heck was that?*

He'd been inside Hel's twisted mind, thinking her thoughts, feeling her cold emptiness, as if any traces of happiness were faint memories lost long ago.

Swinging his legs over the side of his cot, Grayle put his head in his hands and tried to steady his breathing. The wooden floor felt cool on his bare feet. He feared he was losing his mind—hearing mysterious voices in dark caverns and being transported into the mind of a psychotic goddess.

"Get up and get dressed, thief," a gruff voice bellowed from outside his room.

A change of clothes hung on a hook by the door.

Did someone put them there while I was sleeping?

His own clothes were ripped, burned, and pecked full of holes. He stood, peeled off his shirt, catching a whiff of brimstone residue. He scrutinized the cuts on his arms and the bruises splotched across his body. It would have been nice to wash up, but the shower, sink, and humongous tub had been removed, along with the room's other modern comforts.

Comforts a thief doesn't deserve, I guess.

He layered on a pair of thick woollen pants, a knee-length tunic, and a grey cloak, which covered him from head to toe. He was sweating and itchy even before the door opened, releasing him from his prison.

Four guards waited outside. Together they marched him down several halls, joining Sarah as she stepped from her room. Dark circles rimmed her eyes. She hadn't slept well either.

She straightened the folds of a blue tunic that reached down to her ankles. The flash of a sword blade caught Grayle's eye. Next, she slipped her arms through the leather straps of her shield, carrying it like a backpack over her shoulders. Both sword and shield disappeared under a grey cloak she fastened around her neck.

"Are we traveling to Mordor to destroy a ring?" Grayle muttered, trying to scratch an itch just out of reach.

"It'll be cold where we're going," she answered bluntly, still refusing to make eye-contact. "And we'll be blending in."

"Where exactly is this Baldersted?"

"It's remote… up in Lapland."

"That's near the Arctic Circle!" He suddenly felt under-dressed.

She nodded and started down the passageway.

Grayle trailed after her. He wanted to say something—something about her mother or maybe apologize for not following her advice yesterday. But something told him this wasn't the time.

No breakfast was offered before their departure. Even though he was famished, Grayle didn't think he'd be able to eat. He wanted to get this mission… quest… whatever… over with. The sooner he got his hands on the next runestone, the sooner he'd get to the Eye of Odin.

And then I'll finally have the answers I'm looking for.

"This way." Sarah took him outside and followed a path into the overgrown forest circling Midgard.

Grayle squinted into the misty morning light. The fresh air felt good after being held captive for the better part of twelve hours in his tiny prison.

They came to a stairway winding down a deep ravine. Sarah dismissed the guards before starting their descent.

Grayle calculated each step carefully. The morning dew had turned the stairs slippery, and his long cloak kept flapping at his feet, threatening to trip him.

"Is there a reason why Hel would be angry at the gods?" he asked, the damp chill reminding him of his latest dream.

Sarah stopped to look at him. Her eyes narrowed. "Well, they *were* responsible for chaining her father to a rock."

"Besides that."

She started walking again. "All I know is that Loki had three children: Jormungand, Fenrir, and Hel. The gods were warned that these three could bring disaster upon them."

"What kind of disaster?"

"Ragnarok, an event the Vikings believe will bring about the end of the world. To prevent this from happening, Odin flung Jormungand into the sea, Fenrir was bound with magical chains, and Hel was banished to Helheim."

"I'd say that's a pretty good reason for her to be angry," Grayle said.

"I guess. I haven't really given it much thought. Why do you ask?" Sarah gave him another uneasy look.

"I was just wondering why she'd actually want to destroy the world. Seems like overkill, even for a goddess of death. I mean, she could just be searching for the Eye to free her father, right?"

"I doubt it," Sarah said. "Even if that were the case, if Loki gets loose, it's been foretold he will lead armies against the other Norse gods. It was fated that the gods would lose this battle, sending the world into darkness."

"But why would Loki want to destroy the world?"

"Same reason as Hel... revenge. He's convinced that wiping out the gods of Asgard is the best way to make that happen. That's why we need to find the next runestone before she does."

Grayle knew she was right. What he felt while inside Hel's mind wasn't a yearning to free her father. It was vengeance... utter retribution for what the gods had done to her. He shivered at the memory of Hel's thoughts and the disembodied voices. But a part of him understood the goddess's anger—even sympathised with her. It was anger born from hopelessness. Grayle knew what that felt like.

The ground flattened when they reached the bottom of the staircase. Pushing through a copse of evergreen trees, he trailed Sarah to the shores of a large, crystal-clear pond. Six giant, roughly chiselled monoliths were placed in a half circle around the shoreline. Smaller boulders lay inside the water, creating a ring within a ring circling the pool. Fifty yards away, the waterfall Grayle had seen during his climb to the Great Hall cascaded from a rocky gorge and flowed into the pool.

Brenna, Onem, and Haakon were waiting next to a stone platform stretching over the water. Lothar stood among them.

"What is *he* doing here?" Sarah asked.

"In order to further his warlock training, it was decided Prince Lothar would benefit from this experience," Haakon said, not sounding overly convinced.

The prince grinned from ear to ear, obviously pleased at joining the group.

The High Lord shook his head and turned to Onem. "They will need to emerge a fair distance from Baldersted."

"Agreed," the old man said, but Lothar budged ahead of him and hopped across a series of stepping stones to the platform overlooking the pool.

"I will conjure the bifrost," he insisted, lacing his fingers together and cracking his knuckles dramatically. He spread his arms over the water and proceeded to chant a spell.

The water inside the inner ring of stones began to stir, slowly at first, then steadily faster. Foam began to froth along the edges, and a mist floated from the churning water. The funnel of a whirlpool spun to life. A glow emanated from somewhere deep below. Puzzled, Grayle leaned over the edge. Images of ice and blowing snow shimmered in the spinning vortex. Then, without warning, a rainbow shot skyward, streaking from the funnel with a whoosh. It arched northward over the cliff and disappeared into the growing clouds.

Grayle stepped back in time to keep from being drenched by the rainbow's wake. Its colors glistened and reverberated with the low thrum of some mysterious power.

"Not bad—even if I do say so myself," Lothar said, flashing a superior smile at Sarah.

"Why can't we just appear in the middle of town?" Brenna asked.

"The people of Baldersted do not take kindly to witches and warlocks," the Loremaster explained. "They've sided with the Inquisition in the past. How would it look if the four of you suddenly appeared in the city out of thin air? You will not be welcomed, so make your visit short and do not draw attention to yourselves. That is also why you are not to use magic while in the city. Understood?"

They nodded, all except Grayle.

"Wait a second, wait a second." He held up his hands, trying to understand. "You mean to tell me this rainbow—"

"Bifrost," Onem corrected.

"Whatever. You mean this bifrost is able to transport us hundreds of miles away?"

Lothar laughed. Both he and Brenna looked at him as though he were an idiot.

Grayle ignored them. "Why did we have to take the *Drakkar* from Vancouver if we could've used this thing?" he asked.

Sarah shrugged. "Bifrost gateways can only be conjured from fresh water. Salt, even the amount contained in the oceans, prevents our magic from working effectively." She crossed her arms and gazed at the rainbow. "And I'm not strong enough to conjure a bifrost yet."

Lothar's grin grew wider. "It's also dangerous for any *inexperienced* witch to try. The magic to safely materialize at your destination can only be accomplished by the most skilled magickers." He dug his thumbs into his leather belt. "Without proper training, you might open an exit over a river or a ravine or even thirty thousand feet in the air."

"That's a tremendous comfort," Grayle said sarcastically. "How good is he at conjuring these gateways?" He pointed a thumb toward the prince.

Lothar jumped off the flat stone. "Don't be afraid, little thief. We'll arrive in one piece." He bumped Grayle as he walked by. "But not all of us will make it back," he added under his breath.

Sarah couldn't make out what Lothar had mumbled. She was too preoccupied wondering how he was able to muster so much power. The last time she'd been in Midgard, the prince could barely manage a pulse spell. *And now he's conjuring bifrosts?*

Loremaster Onem interrupted her thoughts. "Sarah. Walk with me," he said, leading her away from the others.

Sarah followed him past the giant monoliths to the far edge of the pool. "Have the Coven and my Caretaker been notified of my mission?" she asked. It wasn't often a witch went on missions without the Coven's consent or without a Caretaker at her side.

"The elf is aware you've been given a new assignment."

She nodded. As much as Grigs annoyed her at times, he was the only family she had.

Sarah turned her attention to Lothar. "I don't think it's a good idea taking the prince," she said. "He's never been on a mission."

Onem shook his head. "It was Haakon's decision—a way to appease Erik's hostilities. Many share his sentiments: that we've become mere shadows of what we once were, a proud and influential civilization. Besides, Lothar needs to begin earning his inheritance at some point. He cannot assume Erik's throne, or that of Midgard, without having at least some adventures worthy of song."

Sarah knew that next to fearlessness and loyalty, Vikings valued bravery above all else. A man who had never proven his courage could never be regarded as a leader. "I understand," she said, but still didn't like the idea of the prince tagging along.

The old man patted her shoulder. "He will need guidance. Mentor him. He may turn out to be of some use in the end. But should you require extra luck, you may need this." He handed her a gold coin.

Sarah's eyes lit up. "Is this what I think it is?" she asked. The coin felt heavy in her palm, twice the size of any conventional coins used in the outside world. "The Romans won't be happy we have an artifact that belongs to—"

"Nonsense," the warlock said, closing Sarah's fingers around the gold piece. "This will help you in your quest. And, when you are finished, it may eventually find its way into their Folklore. You do remember the rules for using it?"

Sarah nodded.

"Good. Don't lose it."

She slid the coin into her tunic pocket.

"And I don't need to remind you to keep an eye on the Hexhunter," Onem added.

Sarah followed his gaze to where Grayle was leaning over the bifrost's spinning funnel, looking sick to his stomach. "We need to give him a chance. He may surprise us," she said.

"He is a Hexhunter and, therefore, cannot be trusted," the old man replied matter-of-factly.

"Then why include him in the mission?"

"For one, you'll have little chance of finding the runestone fragments without him."

"What do you mean?"

The wrinkles on the old warlock's forehead deepened. "Hexhunters have unusual connections to magic. You saw it yourself in the museum when he neared the runestone."

"It began to glow, and new runes emerged," Sarah said.

Onem studied her with his milky eye. "There's more. Just as you can see the auras of Folklorian artifacts, a Hexhunter can be subconsciously drawn to them as well. Hel knows this."

Sarah's eyebrows furrowed. "But how can a person have a connection to something he's impervious to?"

"A good question," he said grimly. "It is a mystery Loremasters have been trying to solve for centuries." He paused, then added, "Do you not think it strange that after a thousand years of no word or sighting, two vital clues to the Eye of Odin's whereabouts are revealed? And that a Hexhunter, a person who can be drawn to the Eye, is suddenly found? We must be cautious. The boy could easily become a liability rather than an ally. If he fails to do as he is instructed, he may be the doom of us all. What do you think he's going to do if he finds the next runestone?"

The thought hadn't crossed Sarah's mind. "He'll help us bring it back to Midgard, where you can keep it safe," she said.

"Are you sure? He doesn't seem like the obedient type. How do you know he won't use it to find the other stones and go after the Eye himself? The three of you would be unable to stop him with magic alone."

Sarah wanted to tell the old warlock he was wrong, but she didn't.

Until now, she had been able to dismiss Grayle being a Hexhunter because he didn't act like one—not that she'd ever encountered one before. But what if the Loremaster was right? What if Grayle kept the runestones in order to find the Eye for himself? She couldn't stand that idea any more than she could stand Hel getting her hands on it.

"He'll do the right thing," she said finally, hoping that saying the words out loud would make her believe them too.

"I wish that were true, but I don't want to leave the success of this mission entirely in the hands of a fifteen-year-old Hexhunter trained in the art of thievery. If you find the next runestone, I think it best you bring it *and* the Hexhunter back to Midgard as soon as possible—even against his will if necessary."

"How do you suggest I do that?" she asked. "It's not like I can *make* him come back with me."

The Loremaster reached over and gently uncovered the hilt of Sarah's sword beneath her cloak.

She jerked away, concealing the weapon again. "No way. I'm not going to force him at sword point. It won't come to that."

"You must be prepared to do what is necessary, no matter the cost. Neither the runestones nor the Hexhunter can fall into Hel's hands. Failure is not an option."

"He'll do the right thing," Sarah repeated, too afraid to look the Loremaster in the eye. "And we *won't* fail."

Grayle watched Sarah and Onem argue back and forth in hushed whispers. He knew they were talking about him.

This whole trip is a mistake. Every fibre in his body told him so, but Odin insisted he come along. *Why? There had to be more qualified people to go on missions like this.*

The god's words still rang in his ears: *"Finding the Eye will lead you to the answers you've been seeking."* He'd wondered if Odin meant it would lead him to his parents, but now he wasn't so sure.

Sarah and the Loremaster rejoined the group. Grayle saw her cast a nervous glance his way.

Haakon stepped forward with three small pouches. He handed one each to Brenna, Lothar, and Sarah. "You may need money during your quest." Coins jingled as they attached the pouches to their belts.

"I don't get one?" Grayle asked.

"You can always steal what you need, thief," Lothar said. "That's the only reason you're on this quest."

"And here's a copy of the runes," Haakon added quickly. "They could prove useful when dealing with the Hex." He passed a scroll to Sarah. She tucked it inside her tunic. "Good luck to you all. We do not need to repeat how important your mission is. Get the information from the Hex and find the next runestone. If death finds you, may it take you quickly before your place in Valhalla is taken."

"That's the worst pep talk ever," Grayle muttered.

They all turned, scowling at him.

"Well, it was."

Onem cleared his throat. "Let the All-Father guide your steps and speed your safe return."

"See—that sounds better."

The Loremaster gestured toward the bifrost. "We will remain here and stand at the ready if you require assistance."

"I'll take Grayle through," Sarah said, coming up beside him. "Hold on to me, and we'll jump in feet first."

Lothar climbed onto the stone platform. The rainbow glistened a few feet away. "Yes, make sure you hold the little thief's hand." He laughed and jumped, disappearing into the mist. The rainbow fluctuated like a bedsheet rippling in the wind. Brenna went next. As if plunging from a ten-meter platform, she took a deep breath, pinched her nose, and jumped in.

Grayle hoisted himself onto the flat stone. He gulped, gazing into the maelstrom spinning before him. "Have you gone through a bifrost before?" he asked Sarah, helping her onto the platform.

"No."

"Then how do you—"

"Just trust me." She put her arms around him. "Don't get any bright ideas. I'm still mad at you," she said.

Grayle linked his hands behind her waist. It felt awkward. He had never hugged or been hugged by anyone before. He wasn't big on people touching him. He thought differently when he felt her warmth against him. Smelling the sweet perfume drift from her neck and the shampoo lingering in her hair, he suddenly felt self-conscious. He hadn't showered for two days.

I must stink, he thought.

"Ready? We'll jump on three," Sarah called over his shoulder. "One… two…"

Grayle took a deep breath.

"Three."

Chapter 26

Grayle faltered at the last moment, causing him and Sarah to plunge clumsily into the mist. He sucked in a startled breath, anticipating his splash into the icy water. It never came. He felt a lifting sensation instead, followed by a rumbling whoosh like being caught in a waterfall.

Daring to open his eyes, Grayle saw the ring of stones quickly shrink to pebbles as he and Sarah rocketed skyward, hurtling along the bifrost bridge. Sarah clung to his neck. He wouldn't have minded so much if she weren't choking him. Grayle screwed his eyes shut again, the twisting making him queasy. Just when he thought what little he had in his stomach was about to make an unwelcome return, a frigid burst of air and a brilliant light stunned his senses. The spinning settled.

They materialized, falling into a steep, snow-covered embankment, tumbling and tossing over one another. Cold seeped into Grayle's clothes and shoes, chilling him to the bone. Sarah screamed in his ear. He held her tight, knowing the more compact they were, the less chance they had of injuring an outstretched arm or wayward leg. They rolled to a stop at Brenna's and Lothar's feet.

"Very graceful," the prince said, standing over them.

Grayle loosened his protective grip. Sarah pushed him away.

"What part of *on three* don't you understand?" she yelled, glaring at him.

"Excuse me for not being an expert in magic bridges," he croaked, his stomach still churning.

"What happened?" Brenna asked. The blond witch offered a hand and helped Sarah to her feet.

"Nothing," Sarah muttered and shook the snow from her cloak.

Grayle sat up. The terrain around him was largely void of color. Shades of white, grey, and brown marked where rolling snow dunes and rocks peeped through the mist. Wind-driven snowflakes obscured most everything else, but he could tell they'd emerged on top of a mountain. Blurred above them, two snow-covered peaks towered, and low-lying clouds shrouded whatever lay below.

"Baldersted is down there somewhere?" he shouted over the howling wind.

Sarah nodded, readjusting the shield under her cloak. "Would've been nice if we were a little closer, though," she directed toward Lothar.

The prince shrugged, refusing to offer an explanation or an apology. "It will take another two hours to get there," he said. "We better be going."

They set off with Lothar taking the lead, followed by Sarah, Grayle, and Brenna. The blond witch waited for Grayle to walk on ahead, clearly not trusting him to bring up the rear.

The snow reached their knees, making each step a workout. Angry clouds loomed overhead. Thunder shook the ridge. In a matter of minutes, all Grayle could see was white, blowing snow. He shivered as a barrage of wind sliced into him. The sleet stung his face like a thousand tiny daggers.

"Charming place," he grumbled, leaning into the blizzard and shielding his eyes.

At Gloomshroud, he'd been taught orienteering skills and how to survive in the wilderness. He learned to read direction based on lichen growing on tree trunks, tell time by the position of the sun, learn what could be eaten to stay alive, and make a shelter in almost any environment. But up in this inhospitable place, in the cold, above the tree line, where the sun hid behind dark clouds and no features offered shelter, survival would be difficult if not impossible.

They traveled in silence for nearly half an hour before the storm subsided, making it easier to breathe and to see where they were going. A jumble of broken trees and snow-covered boulders formed the edge of a ravine, blocking their path.

"It would be easier if we went down there," Lothar said, pointing to the bottom of the gorge where the ground levelled off.

"There might be crevasses hidden beneath the surface," Sarah warned. Her breath bloomed in icy clouds over her shoulder.

Lothar crossed his arms. "It's my decision. I'm leading this group, and I say we go that way."

"What makes you think you're in charge? I've been on more missions than you," she said.

"Royal authority." The boy straightened to his full height, which was still two inches shorter than Sarah.

"If you two can give it a rest, you might want to take a look at these." Brenna pointed to three sets of rounded depressions in the snow, moving in a pattern up the slope and beyond the horizon. They were too uniform and straight to have occurred naturally.

Footprints.

"We're not alone," Brenna warned, scouting the area nervously.

"They're fresh," Grayle said, kneeling down to take a closer look. "Made maybe... fifteen, twenty minutes ago."

"How would you know, thief?" Lothar scoffed.

Grayle's eyes narrowed. "Because I've actually been in the wilderness... without escorts to coddle me."

"Why, you impudent—" Lothar reached for his sword.

"Hey!" Sarah got between them. She waited until the prince withdrew his hand from his weapon then turned back to Grayle. "You sure these are fresh?"

Grayle nodded. "Notice the degradation along the edges of each footprint. They're rounded from the wind but not as shallow as they would be, had they been made one or two hours ago. And"—he pointed inside one of the prints—"there's about twenty minutes worth of snow inside each track. That means these footprints were made during the storm, not before." He stood and put his hands on his hips. "These prints are bigger than anything I've ever seen. What could've made them?"

Brenna's voice trembled. "They belong to Jotun—Frost Giants."

"Makes sense—Jotunheim isn't far from here," Sarah said. "We better get off the mountain. The gorge is our fastest option."

They moved quickly, picking their way down slippery boulders and twisted logs. Whether on purpose or not, Lothar let Sarah take the lead. No sooner had they reached the bottom of the ravine than Grayle heard a faint, rhythmic echo. At first, he thought it might be residual thunder from the passing storm, but when he peered back to the summit, something moved in the dissipating clouds.

He squinted, unsure if what he saw was real.

On a mass of snow arching over the ridge stood three gray-skinned giants, nearly twenty feet tall. Even from this distance, Grayle noticed their blue beards and animal furs wrapped around their waists. One had a helmet with massive horns sticking out from either side. All three seemed at home in the frigid climate.

"C-come, make haste," Lothar cried out. He tried to run but stumbled face first into the snow.

"What are they doing?" Brenna asked nervously.

They watched as each giant hefted an enormous axe over their head then let it crash down into the deep snow.

Grayle blinked. "They're standing on a cornice..." He recognized the wind-sculpted curl of snow resembling a frozen wave of ice. Only then did he understand the broken trees and giant boulders piled high on each side of the steep valley. In their rush to get down the mountain, he and the others had blundered straight into an avalanche run-out zone.

With a final crack, the Frost Giants dislodged the cornice. It broke free. Huge ice sheets fractured. The force and weight of tumbling snow loosened the weaker layers below. Snow slabs, like broken panes of glass, broke off with an incredible thunder.

"Run!" Sarah shouted.

Grayle struggled after her, kicking his knees high through the snow. He glanced back and swore under his breath. Like a wall of white death, the avalanche plummeted down the slope at speeds nearing a hundred miles per hour. Judging the distance from where they were to the safety of the valley's edge, he knew they'd never make it.

"Sarah, take out your shield... hurry!"

She did what he asked, slipping it free from under her cloak.

"Make it big… really big!"

She put her free hand over the shield and whispered the growth spell. It grew to the size of a large satellite dish. Too heavy for her to hold, it plopped flat onto the snow.

"Everyone, get on," Grayle said.

The shield tilted as Sarah and Brenna climbed in. Grayle rushed over to where Lothar still struggled to gain his footing but only managed to dig himself deeper into the snow.

"Very graceful," Grayle muttered, grabbing the prince by the scruff of the neck and tossing him onto the shield. He gave it a push before jumping on himself.

The shield quickly gained momentum. The debris of trees and rocks on either side of the run-out zone became an unintelligible blur.

"Give me a sword," Grayle yelled.

Sarah passed him one.

He dug the blade into the snow. Barely offering enough resistance, Grayle had to put his entire weight on it, driving the blade deep into the snowpack. Using it like a rudder, they bounced over the uneven icepack.

"Look out!" Brenna screamed.

A giant boulder loomed ahead.

Grayle cursed. The wind tore the words from his mouth. At the speed they were going, they'd hit the boulder like a fly on a windshield. He shouldered the rudder hard to the right. They swerved, missing the rock by inches. Grayle had to be careful. Coming too close to the ravine's slope meant smashing into more boulders or being skewered alive by jutting tree trunks.

The cold raked Grayle's face. The rushing wind stung his eyes, causing them to tear up, blurring his vision. He wiped them on his sleeve just in time to see the snow drop away ahead—a crevasse, a deep crack in the ice-sheet.

"Hold on!" he shouted.

With only a split second to react, he shifted his weight onto the shield's rear edge, causing the front to tip up. Someone screamed—Grayle could've sworn it was Lothar. Their speed and the shield's upward angle cleared the narrow gap and deflected off the far edge with a back-jarring smack. The impact caused Grayle to bite down on his tongue. He tasted blood.

Sliding on a patch of sheer ice, the shield lurched and accelerated even faster. Grayle leaned on the sword. It chattered violently on the hard surface. With no softer snow for friction, they spun wildly as if caught on some nightmarish tea-cup amusement-park ride.

Lothar squealed, "I'm too young to die! I'm too young to die!"

The sword found leverage again, ploughing into a snow drift and caking their faces with powder.

Cutting into the dune blind, Grayle tried to steady their descent, hoping the way ahead was clear.

It wasn't.

After wiping the snow from his eyes, he saw the run-out zone drop off for a second time. He caught his breath, resisting the urge to hurl himself out of the speeding sled. The sword wedged into a groove and ripped out of his hands. Grayle cursed out loud. He thrust both hands into the snow in a futile attempt to slow their descent. He wasn't strong enough. With no way to stop or steer, he braced for death.

They went over.

Weightlessness sent his stomach to his throat. Just as quickly, the shield crashed down hard and then was airborne again. This happened several times, torturing their bodies with jolt after jolt.

Grayle turned his head. They were shooting over multiple crevasses, each lower than the last, forming an icy stairway down the mountainside. Just when he thought his body couldn't take another pounding, the valley levelled off.

"I n-need... another... s-s-sword!" he managed between chattering teeth and a bloody tongue.

Sarah pulled Lothar's blade from its scabbard and was about to hand it to him when the ravine suddenly bottlenecked.

Grayle set his jaw.

A tree crossed the narrowing gulley.

"Get down!" he yelled.

They passed under it, barely keeping their heads.

Then a deafening roar rumbled behind them.

The avalanche.

As quickly as they careered down the mountain, the avalanche was faster. It surged, encroaching on either side of their sled, threatening to overtake them. In a few more seconds, they'd be encased in a frigid white tomb.

Grayle's heart pounded hard enough to burst through his chest. *We're not going to make it.*

Sarah, who had clung to his waist until then, struggled to her knees.

"What are you—" Grayle began.

The shield jostled.

Sarah shifted her balance to keep from tumbling out only to fall shoulder first into Grayle's face.

"Mmpff!" he protested.

She screamed, "Vanya!" and the magical shockwave he'd felt during their car chase in Vancouver now exploded behind him.

Using the tumbling ice to push off, the pulse deflected back and thrust the sled forward, keeping them ahead of certain death.

"I. Can't. Do. This. For much. Longer!" Sarah shouted, almost inaudible against the fearsome noise.

Staying in the run-out zone would kill them. Grayle had to get them out. He peered over Sarah's shoulder. Off to the right, a slough of snow trailed up the embankment like a ramp, free of fallen trees or boulders. In a split-second reaction, he veered. Grayle gritted his teeth, the strain to his arms excruciating.

"Hold on," he shouted.

Sarah obeyed, hugging her arms and pressing her cheek against his.

The shield burst up and over the snow bank. Time seemed suspended in that moment. Grayle went weightless, lifting off the sled with Sarah wrapped tightly to him. The mountainside dropped out from under them, causing all four to freefall for several seconds. With a stab of terror, Grayle expected to plummet over another cliff or shatter his bones against rocks. Soft powder swallowed him instead, finding its way up every sleeve, ear, and nostril.

The rest of the avalanche crashed against the run-out zone's barrier behind them, forcing the cascading snowpack further down the ravine and away from their sprawled-out bodies.

The four dug themselves free and tested for broken bones.

All intact.

So was the shield, sticking halfway out of the snow bank like a half moon a few yards away.

"I was wrong." Grayle coughed and spat snow from his mouth.

"About what?" Sarah asked, catching her breath.

"Stealing the shield was a *great* idea."

Grayle and Sarah couldn't control their laughter. Their terror transformed into a strange elation, leaving Brenna and Lothar wondering if they'd lost their minds.

Chapter 27

"We've been betrayed," Brenna muttered.

Sarah and the others had trudged across the snowy landscape in uneasy silence since their terrifying sled ride down the mountain. On the bright side, the crazy ride had cut their travel time in half. The sudden appearance of Jotun, however, left Sarah wondering what awaited them next.

"I think you're right," she said. She hated the thought of a traitor in Midgard, but it was the only possible explanation. How else could the Frost Giants have known of their mission to Baldersted?

Lothar had summoned the bifrost—pushing his way past Onem to do so. Had he chosen their destination on purpose for an ambush?

He's not that good of a warlock, Sarah reminded herself. Then again, before conjuring the bifrost, she'd never known him to harness such power. *Could he be faking his true talents?*

And what about Brenna? Did she have the skill to tamper with a bifrost? Even if she did, how would she have managed to communicate with the Frost Giants?

"If there actually is a traitor then we don't have much time," Sarah said. "Whoever's involved knows the Hex has information we need."

Brenna glared at Grayle. "I say we go back. There's no telling who or what else might be waiting for us."

"Hey, don't look at me," he said. "I don't have any magic, and no one trusts me. I bet these Frost Giants feel the same as all of you."

Sarah couldn't help giving him a playful nudge, letting him know that wasn't the case. After their near-fatal descent, she'd stayed by his side, unable to stay angry at him, especially after his quick thinking saved all their lives. She saw him differently now, not as thief, or a means to an end to get what she needed. Not even as a Hexhunter. She recognized him as someone who could survive in this world—the world of Folklore. And she needed him to. If they were going to find the next runestone, she needed someone who could survive Hel-hounds and avalanches, maybe even more dangerous things than that.

Brenna shook her head. "Whatever. But going back is an option we may have to—"

"I will not return to Midgard empty-handed!" Lothar shouted. "All we need to do is find the Hex and get the information."

The outburst brought uncomfortable looks.

"As much as I hate to admit it, he's right," Sarah said. "This is our only chance to get the next runestone. If we stop here, if we turn back, we might as well be handing the Eye over to Hel."

"And we have to get the information fast," Grayle added. "If those giants knew we were coming, they'd also know we're heading to Baldersted."

Sarah raised an eyebrow, not expecting him to sound like part of the team.

"Fine," Brenna snapped. "Then let's get what we came for and get out of here."

*　　*　　*

At last they crested a rise and spotted a town along the shoreline of a fjord below. Baldersted nestled in a haphazard layout of stone houses and narrow streets. A third of the village extended over the frozen water, supported by a hundred posts dug deep into the sea bed. Wisps of smoke drifted from chimneys, and a dusting of snow had settled on the rooftops like icing sugar. The village looked peaceful, hardly the place Grayle expected to find a Hex.

"What exactly is a Hex anyway?" he asked, fingering melted snow from his ear.

"Hexes were witches who used their magic to kill," Sarah said. "We draw our magic from the ambient energy nature provides us. But killing for the sake of killing goes against the laws of nature. The more innocent the life that's taken, the darker a Hex's connection with her magic becomes."

"You should not be telling him these things," Lothar said.

"Why?"

"He's an Outlander."

"So? You'd rather he *not* know what we're up against?"

The prince never answered.

"But why would a Hex live in a place that hates magic?" Grayle asked. "Wouldn't the townspeople hunt her down?"

"A Hex draws dark energy from the fear of others," Brenna explained. "A town without knowledge of witches can't generate the same kind of terror in its people or, in this case, their children."

Grayle swallowed. "Does she really eat them—the children, I mean?"

Sarah nodded. "Yeah. To everyone else, she may look like a nice old lady, somebody's grandmother—the perfect disguise to lure unsuspecting kids."

"I heard she can put a hypnotic spell on them," Brenna added. "They don't even know they're with a Hex until it's too late."

"So how will *we* recognize her?" Grayle asked.

Sarah tapped a gloved finger under her eye. "I'll be able to spot her."

Right. He'd forgotten she could see auras. "So how does a thief figure into all of this? What do I need to steal?"

"Nothing… yet," Sarah said. "First we need the information the Hex can provide. Hopefully it'll be enough to figure out where the next runestone fragment is hidden."

"And what if she doesn't want to tell us?" he asked.

"Then we become more persuasive," Lothar said, exposing the sword beneath his cloak.

It wasn't long until Baldersted's fortifications loomed before them. They were as tall as those surrounding Midgard but seemed thinner and flimsier in comparison. A patchwork of stone and tree trunks speckled the outer layer, evidence the town had repelled several attacks throughout its history. Armored soldiers stood guarding its gates and battlements. They watched stone faced as a steady caravan of farmers and ox carts trundled into the city.

Grayle and the others slipped into the procession, following a cart filled with steaming manure.

"Ugh." Brenna pulled her hood over her nose. "This whole quest is beginning to reek," she grumbled. "Couldn't we have found a vegetable or hay cart to hide behind?"

Children darted past them. They giggled, playing hide-and-go-seek and keep away between the wagons. Grayle hated to think what would happen if hordes of grey-skinned giants descended on their town. "Shouldn't we let the people know the Frost Giants are coming?" he said uneasily.

Brenna grimaced. "And cause wide-scale panic? They'll ask us how we know, and then what? We tell them we came from the top of the mountain through a bifrost?" She shook her head adamantly. "No. We get what we came for and leave, drawing as little attention to ourselves as possible—just like the Loremaster wanted us to."

"They're innocent. It's wrong not telling them," Grayle said.

Lothar humphed. "These people once helped the Inquisition hunt down witches and warlocks. A little giant attack is small payback in comparison."

Grayle was about to argue when Sarah intervened. "Our sled ride bought us some time. We can find the Hex, warn the locals, and still get out of Baldersted before the giants arrive."

They followed the parade of creaking wagons and clopping horse hooves into the town square, an open expanse in the town's center surrounded by half-timbered buildings and a large, ornate clock tower. Hundreds of smiling and laughing faces filled the square. Music played from every corner, blending together in a cacophony of horns, flutes, and stringed instruments.

Trailing behind Sarah in single file, they squeezed past the packed bodies filling the square. Sarah headed along the plaza's edge, where vendors had set up shop, selling barbecued reindeer, baked pretzels, and soup steaming in cooking pots.

The festive atmosphere and sheer number of people swirling around him struck Grayle as odd. He figured a town with a child-snatching Hex should feel glummer. Instead, he saw minstrels singing and townspeople kicking up their heels as though a cannibal witch was the last thing on their minds.

"This isn't at all what I expected."

"You're a master of observation," Lothar muttered.

"He's right. Something's off," Brenna said. "Why are they celebrating?"

"Haven't you heard?" said a woman within earshot of their conversation. She wore a shawl wrapped around her head, drawing attention to her ugly, pointed nose and high cheekbones. She motioned to where townspeople lingered around a raised platform surrounding the charred remains of an old oak tree. "After months of searching, the Hex was finally caught this morning. Her execution at noon will finally see this terrible blight to our city come to an end."

Something placed below the platform caught Grayle's eye. It was a cage. An old woman cowered inside. Her hair and clothes were smeared with egg yolk and splattered tomatoes. She shivered pathetically while onlookers hurled vicious insults and more rotten vegetables.

"Oh, no," Sarah whispered.

"What is it?" asked Brenna.

"The woman… she's normal… I mean, her aura's normal. She's not the Hex."

Lothar rubbed his hands together. "Good. That means she's still out there for us to find."

Sarah shot him a disgusted look. "There's nothing good about it. They're going to burn an innocent person."

"Innocent?" The same woman eavesdropped again. "I'm afraid you're terribly mistaken. That witch was caught red-handed with a missing child the day before yesterday. Luckily, the lad was still alive. Any longer and he would've been eaten."

Then her shrivelled eyes narrowed and scrutinized each of them. "You're not sympathizers, are you? Friends of magic?"

"Of course not," Sarah said. "I hope the witch burns." She spat on the ground for added effect and nudged the others to keep moving.

They passed a stall displaying crude carvings of witches tied to stakes, spray repellent to ward off magic, and bundles of hay.

A leathery-looking merchant inside yelled, "Bushels for sale! Come get your bushels. Make sure the witch burns good and proper. Please," the man implored, noticing Grayle and the others hurrying by, "buy a bushel to help support the families of the Hex's victims."

Grayle could see Sarah's shoulders vibrating angrily. She stomped past the vendor without saying a word, knifing her way between people. The others had a hard time keeping up. She finally stopped in a deserted alcove.

"Lothar and I will go looking for *her*," Sarah said through clenched teeth, careful not to mention *witch*, *Hex* or anything else that might be overheard. "And you two need to free the innocent woman from being burned to death."

Grayle didn't like the idea. If Lothar was the traitor, she'd be in danger. He put his hand on her arm. "I should go with you. You might need a thief," he said, trying to make his case.

"No." Her hand slipped over his and squeezed his fingers. "We have to go. If the Jotun are on their way, we might have another half hour, tops. It's better this way."

Lothar scowled at Grayle. "What if he tries to get away?"

Grayle spread his arms and looked around. "Where am I going to go, huh? I'm near the Arctic Circle with no way to get home… come to think of it, I don't have a home to go back to. I don't have anything except"—he turned to face Sarah—"you guys."

"I'll watch him," Brenna said. "He won't be going anywhere."

"Not exactly the company I was hoping for," Grayle mumbled.

"Stay together, you two," Sarah whispered. Then, leaning in close, she added, "Grayle, no reckless behavior. Got it? I can't have you going all Mr. Invincible. You're too important to the mission, so be careful."

"Aw... you're starting to like having me around."

She punched his shoulder. "Be serious. Stay together. And. Stay. Out. Of. Trouble," she said, poking him in the chest. "There could be worse things hunting us than Frost Giants."

With that, she and Lothar melted into the crowd.

Grayle gave Brenna an anxious glance. "That girl has a knack for making me nervous."

Chapter 28

"Dealing with a Hex is dangerous business," Sarah reminded Lothar. The pair had made their way out of the town square and onto one of several side streets branching from the city center. "They prey on the fear and despair of others. It makes them stronger. So we need to control our emotions. Are you even listening to me?"

The prince sighed. "Yes."

Sarah didn't believe him. He seemed focused on everything but her: the houses, alleys, the sky—either he had a serious case of attention deficit disorder or he was choosing to ignore her on purpose. She started regretting choosing him to come along. But if she had left Grayle and Lothar together, the two would've been at each other's throats in seconds. If she'd taken Grayle, the Hex would've sensed he was a Hexhunter. Then not only would they not get the information they needed, but Grayle's life would be in danger.

"Loremaster Onem gave me instructions to teach you while we're out here," Sarah said. "Apparently you need some guidance."

"I'm not some child to be coddled. I'm Lothar, son of Erik the Red."

You're an idiot and the son of an even bigger idiot, she wanted to say. "Do you have any idea what we're up against?" she asked.

"No, do you? Have you ever gone after a Hex before?"

Sarah opened her mouth, but couldn't say anything in her defence. She'd never crossed paths with a Hex.

"That's what I thought," Lothar said, his usual smugness returning to his face. "So which house do you think belongs to her?"

Sarah peered down the cobblestone road. Houses were cramped together, practically leaning on each other, blocking out much of the flat spring daylight. "Not sure. None of them are projecting an aura."

The prince walked on ahead. "Then we'll have to go knocking on each door."

"Wait," Sarah called after him.

The prince spun around. "We can't wait! Every moment brings the others closer to finding the next runestone, and if they get to it first—"

"I know. It can mean the end of us all," Sarah said, surprised at his sudden empathy.

Lothar gave her a puzzled look. "What are you talking about? If others find it first, I won't have the glory of returning it to my father."

"Is that all you care about? The glory?"

He shrugged. "What else is there? So I'll knock on these doors, and you knock on those."

Sarah clenched her fists. It took all her composure not to punch the pompous prince in the head. She let out a slow, drawn-out breath. "Look… knocking on doors will only arouse suspicion and won't help us find a Hex who's been concealing herself for who knows how long. Besides, what are you going to say? 'I'm looking for a thousand year old Hex; are you her?' We need to use our heads if we're going to find her quickly."

Lothar shrugged again as if to say, *Whatever*.

Sarah let it go and focused on the street ahead. It meandered in an S-pattern with side streets angling in both directions. "The Hex eats children and lives off of the misery of others. She'd most likely be living in the foulest part of town, right? And evil as old as hers leaves a trace. Chances are she's put a camouflage spell on her home to hide its true features. But the spell would be infectious, spreading to the surrounding buildings like a virus."

"But there are way too many streets and houses," Lothar argued. "We'd be lucky to find her in the next day or two."

Sarah snapped her fingers. "Luck. That's it." She reached into her tunic pocket and produced the gold coin Onem had given her before they entered the bifrost.

"What's that?"

"It's an old Roman coin." Sarah held it up for him to see. The crude relief of a man wearing a crown of laurel leaves was stamped on the front. It was a miracle it hadn't fallen out during their harrowing sled ride. "It gives its owner luck in making decisions when there are two choices to be made. The Loremaster gave it to me before we left."

Lothar snatched it from her hand. "How does it work?"

"Hey, give it back."

The prince held the coin out of her reach. "Something this valuable belongs in *my* possession," he said, as if daring Sarah to question his royal authority again.

"Fine," she said, backing off.

"So how does it work?" he repeated, mesmerized by the shiny object.

"You stand at an intersection, like we are now. Hold the coin out in front of you and ask which way to go."

"You mean like… we're looking for the Hex's house. Heads we go left, tails we go right?"

She nodded. "Now flip it."

The prince tossed the coin in the air, letting it clink and settle on the uneven cobblestones.

Heads.

"All right then," Lothar said, pointing left. "We go this way." He picked up the gold piece and reached for the leather pouch underneath his cloak. "What the…" His hands searched along his belt.

"What is it?" Sarah asked.

"My money… it's been stolen!"

* * *

Grayle's mouth watered as he fingered through a handful of copper coins. He handed over the required amount and grabbed a warm pretzel from the baker's hands.

"How can you be thinking of food at a time like this?" Brenna asked, not looking very impressed.

Grayle shrugged. "Out-sledding an avalanche builds appetite." He slathered mustard on the pastry. "Besides"—he took a bite, and the salty outer layer crunched in his mouth—"we skipped breakfast this morning. Want some?"

Brenna shook her head and crossed her arms. "Where did you even get the money to pay for that?"

Grayle smiled and raised his arms. A coin pouch jingled from his belt. "Prince Lothar can be very generous."

"You stole it from him?"

"His dagger, too." Grayle smirked. "Hey, he told me to steal what I needed—and I needed his money."

Brenna scrunched her face and looked away, refusing to say anything else.

Grayle ignored her reaction and took another bite.

Before he was caught and sent to Gloomshroud, Grayle had never given a second thought about the banks, jewellery stores, and homes he'd stolen from. He'd convinced himself the money belonged to overpaid CEOs or members of the mafia. The excuses became more elaborate, to the point where he believed his own lies and stopped feeling anything for the victims he burgled. Ultimately, he deflected responsibility onto Zito for what had happened. Deep inside though, he knew he only had himself to blame.

The pretzel suddenly lost its flavor.

Tossing the pastry aside, Grayle dragged his mind back to their current problem. He focused on the market square. Somehow, they had to get closer to the cage and find a way to free the old woman. The more he analyzed their situation, the more impossible it seemed.

Brenna tapped her foot nervously. "There's no way we can free the woman with all these people around."

Several heads turned in their direction.

"Keep your voice down," Grayle hissed, "or it'll be us burning at the stake, too."

She had a point though. *This isn't going to be like breaking into a bank.*

More costumed dancers, dressed in animal furs and feathers, made their way through the crowd. Behind them, a masked jester juggled balls in time with bells fastened to his elbows and ankles.

Grayle's attention wandered past the jester to where a large figure shouldered his way through the crowd. The blood drained from his face. He recognized him instantly.

It was hard not to.

Caine's bodyguard—the ultimate fighter once known as the Belgian Brawler—was heading straight for them.

Chapter 29

Sarah and Lothar made steady progress, thoroughly checking every nook and cranny along Baldersted's tangled streets. But despite using the coin a second time to reduce their search area, the task of finding the Hex still seemed too daunting.

Sarah hoped Grayle and Brenna were faring better. Freeing the old woman would be difficult—maybe impossible. But she couldn't dwell on that now. She had her own job to do. It wasn't long before she and Lothar came to another crossroad.

"I'm going to use the coin again," the prince said eagerly. Using the magical gold piece had been the only thing that calmed him after discovering his pouch *and* dagger had been stolen. Sarah suspected Grayle was behind it, hiding a smile when Lothar made the connection.

"Heads we go left; tails we go right." Lothar tossed the coin in the air and let it tumble along the cobblestones until it came to rest tail side up. The coin suddenly lost its lustre as if an inner power had been snuffed out.

"What happened to it?" he asked.

"That was your last toss," Sarah said. "It won't work for you anymore." She plucked it from the ground and let it settle in her hand. Its golden sheen returned. "Oh, didn't I tell you? A person can only use it three times."

"What? That's not fair!"

"Crying about it won't change anything. Your flips are done."

Lothar pressed his lips together until they turned white. "You tricked me," he said, stabbing a finger at her.

Sarah tucked the coin into her tunic pocket and took the side street to the right. "I seem to remember you grabbing the coin out of my hand," she called over her shoulder. "Here's another lesson: learn everything you can about a magical item before you use it. Thanks for helping, though."

For a second, she thought the prince might conjure a spell against her. He buried his hands in his cloak instead and trailed after her, sulking.

A part of her—a very small part—felt sorry for him. She couldn't imagine the pressure he was under—his entire inheritance, the thrones of Greenland and possibly Midgard, could be at stake. Worse, if he didn't return with a piece of the runestone, he would have to face his father's wrath.

Still doesn't give him the right to be a jerk, she thought. *And with so much depending on his success, how much can I trust him to do what's right for the mission and not just what's right for him?*

In light of everything that had happened, she couldn't trust anyone—except for Grayle. She grinned, thinking how a Hexhunter, a being most lethal to witches, could be her only—

A tremor swept over her like an icy chill.

She stopped abruptly and scanned the length of a deserted side street.

A house at the end caught her eye. It had an aura, shifting between shades of purple and oily black. Sarah moved closer. She'd never experienced aural projections from a Hex before, but she imagined it would look and feel like a greasy stain.

"Pssst. I think I found it," she whispered.

Lothar sauntered across the road. "Doesn't look like the house of a Hex to me," he mumbled.

"Exactly. It's almost too perfect."

Outwardly, the house looked cheerful and inviting. Flower baskets and bright blue painted window shutters decorated the front. Its white-washed exterior practically glowed compared to the neighboring, run-down buildings—the only house on the block children would have felt safe approaching if they needed help, or if a kindly old woman promised them cookies waited inside.

"Well… what are you waiting for?" Lothar went to knock on the door.

"No!" Sarah stepped in front of him. "Not revealing the house's true features is dangerous. What looks like a door can be a trapping curse, pulling unsuspecting visitors into the house." Sarah examined the outer walls more closely then scanned the street, making sure they were alone. "Give me your hand."

The prince hesitated. "What for?"

After duping him with the coin, she couldn't blame him for being suspicious. "Our combined magic can break the Hex's spell," she said.

Lothar reluctantly put his clammy hand in hers.

Concentrating on their flowing energies, she allowed their auras to meld together. She felt a power surge almost instantly, thrumming her magical core like an amplifier. Lothar's magic was more potent than she'd expected.

No wonder he was able to conjure the bifrost... and who knows what else.

She pushed thoughts of his treachery aside and focused on the house. The reveal spell they needed would take more effort than exposing holographic pictures in steam or smoke. Cracking a Hex's camouflage spell not only required power but intense concentration.

"Finta," she said.

Nothing happened.

"Are you channelling your magic?" she asked irritably.

"Yes."

She suspected he wasn't.

"Let's try again. Imagine the house's camouflage melting away," she said, shutting her eyes and directing her thoughts again. This time she accessed his magic, nurtured it, coaxed it to join with hers. She dug deep into their combined magic, channelling it from their linked hands, to her body. Their magic pulsed between them and around them, binding them together, and making them one with the ambient energy so that their power tripled in strength. She projected it towards the house.

"Finta," she repeated.

A cold wind whipped from their auras, tousling Sarah's hair and causing their cloaks to billow. When she opened her eyes, the freezing air had covered the house in a thick layer of ice. It began to shatter into a thousand crystals, falling away like broken glass. Slowly, the house began to reveal itself.

Sarah let go of Lothar's hand and stepped back.

The Hex's true lair was a terrible sight. The outer walls had turned from white to weathered brown. Hordes of termites clustered in areas, eating away at the rotting wood. The windows and flower baskets had disappeared too. A single wooden door on rusted hinges was the only way in or out. The doorknob was a mouth filled with sharp teeth. Metal placeholders jutted from either side of the doorway, but in place of torches, human skulls had been speared on wooden pikes. The eyes, still suspended in their sockets, peered down at them.

Lothar moaned. "Why do I feel like Hansel and Gretel all of a sudden?"

Sarah ignored him. "Whatever happens or whatever you see, let me do the talking." She approached the wooden door and knocked.

No answer.

"M-maybe she isn't h-home."

"No, she is," Sarah said, steeling herself. She knocked again.

They waited.

Sarah heard floorboards creaking. The blood drained from her cheeks. How crazy was it to show up at the door of a known cannibal—on purpose?

The doorknob turned with a squeak.

The door opened.

The head of an old woman poked out. She had a long, crooked nose and a thin-lipped mouth. Her eyes were grey with little pinpricks for pupils. Her face was brown and wrinkled like an apple left in the sun too long. But most frightening weren't the bone earrings dangling from her lobes or the skull of a dead rodent constraining the ends of her white, straw-like braids. It wasn't even the aura oozing around her like greasy sludge. Worst of all was her necklace. Slender bones were bound together on a long leather cord—the finger bones of children.

She smiled wickedly, sending the hairs on Sarah's neck on end.

"I been expecting you," the Hex said in a thick accent.

Sarah was almost too afraid to breathe. "You… you've been waiting for us?"

"Zat is vhat I zaid," the old woman answered. "Vould you like to come inside?"

Sarah's mind screamed *no*, but the mission was too important to stop here. They'd come this far. She had to see it through.

She and Lothar stepped across the threshold. The door creaked shut behind them like a coffin lid.

* * *

Grayle felt a tightening in his gut. Caine's bodyguard began to walk faster, pushing through the crowd like a freight train.

Grayle reached for Brenna's arm.

"Hey…" she said, pulling away.

He held a finger to his lips and, half-crouching, motioned for her to follow. They sneaked out into the busy promenade, weaving past vendors and street performers, finally slipping inside a stall selling cooking pots. Grayle peeked past the stall's awning. The bodyguard towered above everyone. His beady eyes, set deep in his face, scanned the crowd. He wore a cloak several sizes too small and a black T-shirt, revealing biceps the size of cantaloupes. It didn't look like he could feel the cold, or feel anything for that matter.

Grayle ducked into the shop and held his breath as the goon marched by.

Brenna scowled. "You mind telling me what's going on?"

It took a second for Grayle's mouth to obey his thoughts. The words came out slowly. "Back in Vancouver… there was this super-rich guy… Sebastian Caine, the guy they were talking about at the All-Thing. He tried to capture Sarah in the museum." Grayle kept an eye on Mussels as the man continued along the square's perimeter. "Well, that's his bodyguard, which means he's searching for Sarah—or us."

"How did he know we were here?" Brenna asked.

"Not sure." Grayle tried to put the pieces together. "A billionaire like Caine has his sources. Somehow he found out we were in Norway, but he couldn't have known we were in Baldersted, unless…"

"Unless there *is* a traitor," Brenna finished.

Grayle's mouth went dry. The puzzle started to make sense. "It's Lothar—it has to be. And Sarah's with him! We have to warn her."

"What? No way," Brenna said, shaking her head.

"Fine. I'll go alone." He flipped his hood over his head. "I'll be back in a bit."

"No," she fired back. "We can't leave the old woman to die."

"You can save her."

"I can't use my magic here… in front of everyone," she added under her breath. "Sarah can take care of herself, but that woman needs us."

She was right. He had to do something. No one had been there for him when his second fo-rent shackled him to his bed at night or before he was sent to Gloomshroud. He couldn't abandon this innocent person to die.

"All right." He gave in, watching the clock inch closer to noon. "But we have to think of something fast."

Chapter 30

No amount of concentration could tamp down Sarah's fear. The Hex's lair was ripe with it. Once she and Lothar entered, Sarah had gotten the distinct feeling she wasn't the first girl to enter this deathtrap. She felt surrounded by the residual terror left by the auras of frightened children, lured into the evil witch's home, never to see the light of day again. Raising her mental guard, Sarah tried to block them out, but their pain wore down her courage.

The Hex led them into a single room much larger than seemed possible in a house that size. Shelves lined the walls, stacked with spellbooks in a dozen languages and neatly labelled jars filled with floating organs. Sarah noticed another room sectioned off by a beaded curtain in one corner while a cabinet filled with elixir vials towered in the opposite corner. The place had a pungent smell. She suspected it came from the dried herbs and thorny weeds hanging in bunches from the ceiling. She gulped, eyeing a cauldron bubbling over a roaring fireplace. She didn't want to know what might be stewing inside.

They sat at a table covered in a yellowing, tattered cloth. The Hex settled across from them. The bones on her necklace wagged back and forth, as though the children's fingers were warning them to stay away. She pulled a small, ornate vial from her pocket. Opening the cap, a puff of black vapor curled up to her nose. The Hex inhaled deeply, sucking the mist into her nostrils. Bottled fear—somehow the Hex had managed to trap the emotion, contain it—keeping a steady dose at hand.

"May I get you zom tea? Zom biscuits perhaps?" the old witch purred.

"No, thank you," Sarah replied, fighting to keep her voice pleasant. "We only came for information." She knew if she and Lothar ate or drank anything here, they'd be drugged and dead in minutes.

The Hex sat there for a moment, sizing up her two visitors. "Vhat kind of information?"

"We understand you helped Halfdan the Far-Travelled in his search for the Well of Wisdom."

The old witch's face twitched. "Halfdan? Zat is a name I do not know."

"Are you sure?" Lothar cut in.

The Hex never took her eyes off Sarah. "Perhaps I may haf known such a man long ago," she said. "But I am old woman. Ze mind begin to forget, da?"

Sarah had a feeling the old witch was only acting forgetful. "Maybe these will help jar your memories." She pulled the scroll Haakon had given her from beneath her cloak and flattened it on the table. "These are runes taken from a runestone Halfdan smashed into five pieces centuries ago. We've recovered the inscriptions from two fragments; the other pieces are still missing. We were hoping you may know where they are."

The old crone extended a gnarled hand and mumbled a spell. The runes lifted off the parchment and orbited the table like constellations. She scanned the runic letters. "I had wisitor come zis morning," she croaked. "Come in vit Viking runes also and… present. Ask me to translate."

Lothar straightened in his seat. "They had Viking runes as well?" he repeated.

"Da. Came in vit same runes like zese." She tapped the paper.

Sarah held her breath. Someone had beaten them here. "What can you tell us about this visitor?" she asked.

The Hex let out a bored sigh and pushed the scroll aside. The floating runes sucked back into the parchment. "Ze man vas almost too big to fit zrough door."

Sarah risked dropping her mental guard, searching for the visitor's aural echo. Her hopes dropped. *Caine's bodyguard. It had to be.* "What did you tell him… the big man?"

"A zecret," the Hex whispered with an eerie giggle.

Lothar almost jumped out of his seat. "Secret! What secret? I would have you tell me, old woman!"

The dark witch showed no reaction. "To do such a ting, I vould require… payment."

The prince went to reach for his coin pouch, only to remember it had been stolen.

The Hex frowned and clucked her tongue. "I haf no need for gold," she said, guessing Lothar's intentions. A twisted smile revealed her sharpened teeth. A trail of saliva gathered at the edge of her cracked lips as her gaze fell on Sarah. "I vould very much like to bargain for zis young girl."

Sarah's heart leapt to her throat. "Out of the question!"

"Oh, but ozer wisitor give me such vunderful present."

Sarah cringed as the old woman licked her lips.

"Vhat haf you brought me?"

A slight tremor rattled the jars lining the Hex's shelves.

The old witch never noticed. She reached out to stroke Sarah's arm but recoiled the moment her fingers touched her skin. "You haf echo of darkness!" She spat. "You haf been touched by somezing ze ancients haf tvisted."

Sarah jerked her arm away. "What are you talking about?"

"You haf had contact vit a Hexhunter. Vhere is he?"

"Hexhunter?" Lothar's eyes darted from the Hex to her. "What is she talking about, Sarah?"

"I don't know."

"You lie. Vhere is he?"

"Good gods! The thief—is he a Hexhunter, Sarah? Is he?" Lothar pressed.

Sarah wished he'd shut up. He was only making things worse. "I-I don't know what she means." She fought to keep her voice even.

The Hex's eyes glazed with madness. Her pupils dilated into black marbles. "You dare act coy viz me?"

Quicker than Sarah thought possible, the old witch bound from her chair. She pounced on her like a cougar, wrapping her bony fingers around Sarah's throat. Jars tumbled from shelves, spilling their contents everywhere as the Hex rammed her against a wall.

"I need to know vhere he is, child," she hissed, pushing her face close. Her breath reeked of rotten meat. "Ze blood of a Hexhunter vill make me powerful."

Lothar moved to intervene but stopped when the Hex tightened her grip.

"You vill leave here, boy," she said to the prince. "But zis child…" She trailed a sharp fingernail up and down Sarah's cheek. "Vhen she tells me vhat I vant to know, she vill make vunderful lunch guest, da?"

Sarah squirmed in the witch's grasp.

Lothar stood his ground. "I'm not going anywhere until you tell me the location of the next runestone."

The old woman cackled. With remarkable strength, she swung Sarah up and in front of her like a living shield. "You are too late. Ze ozer man knows vhere to go next."

"Tell me now, and *I* will tell you where to find the Hexhunter," the prince offered.

"Don't you dare." Sarah rasped from under the Hex's choke-hold.

The old crone regarded Lothar sharply, then recited:

"Halfdan sought ze All-Fahzer's Eye,
In caverns deep and mountains high,
But in ze capital of ze east,
Ze quest for glory he did zease."

The prince's lips moved silently, committing the verse to memory. "Is that it? That doesn't tell me anything."

"Zhat is vhat I know. Now, vhere is ze Hexhunter? Tell me…" The Hex's fingers tightened around Sarah's jugular, making her wince.

"We left him in the town square." Lothar shrugged. "He's still there, for all I know."

The witch's mouth spread into a wide grin… and kept spreading. "Zat is good. I vill find him… after I haf my lunch." She opened her mouth and unhinged her jaw to the point where it gaped three times wider than a normal human's. Rows of sharp teeth, like those of a shark, unfolded as her mouth grew wider and wider.

Sarah's mind flashed images of evil fairy tale witches devouring children whole. She thrashed but couldn't free herself from the Hex's grip. She felt the cannibal's hot breath on her throat.

"You vill be tasty morsel," the Hex whispered. "Zen I vill have my present for dessert." She glanced into the back room.

Sarah struggled. Her heart pounded, too terrified to focus her magic.

The Hex's mouth gaped open, ready to distend and take a chunk out of her, when a horn sounded. Startled by the interruption, the old witch stopped. Her jaw reattached and shrank back to normal size.

The horn blared again, this time accompanied by heavy thudding. It came from the street. The old woman twisted toward the door, trying to determine who or what dared disrupt her snack time.

The entire house rattled, causing the walls and ceiling to shudder. More jars fell, and dried herbs fluttered from the ceiling. With a thunderous crash, an immense club suddenly tore through the side of the Hex's home. Pieces of wood siding and furniture tumbled everywhere.

Lothar let out a high-pitched squeal and dove beneath the table.

The shock loosened the old woman's grip enough for Sarah to wrench herself free. She hit the floor, looking up in time to see two grey-skinned legs lumbering past what was left of the home's threshold.

The Frost Giants had arrived.

Disoriented, the Hex stumbled over the wreckage.

Sarah saw her chance. "Naur-galad!"

A fireball ignited in her hand. She hurled it at the Hex, catching her by surprise. The fireball twisted in flaming loops, binding her arms and legs to her sides. Before the old witch could manage a counterspell, Sarah pulsed her against the wall. The Hex's head cracked against an upturned shelf, and she slumped to the floor, out cold.

Sarah sank to her knees, coughing. She could still feel the Hex's grip around her throat. How close had she come to death?

Lothar crawled out from under the table, his face ghostly white.

"You filthy little—" Sarah grabbed the prince by the collar. "You were going to leave me!"

"No, I was going to help."

"And how were you going to do that by walking away?"

"W-we have what we came f-for," he sputtered. "Let's get out of here!"

"No," Sarah said, her throat still sore. "We have to put the Hex somewhere where she can't hurt anyone else… at least for a while."

She hopped over the rubble and, taking the old witch by the wrists, dragged her into the room separated by the beaded curtain. It was filled with cabinets and large wooden chests. She opened the nearest crate and stopped.

It was filled with children's clothes—the clothes of the Hex's victims.

Sarah squeezed her eyes shut, fighting back tears.

Such evil. No wonder the Hex was consumed with dark magic.

How can I let a monster like this live?

She wanted to put her hands around the Hex's throat. The echoes of the dead egged her on. Sarah felt their emotions. The fear. The terror of their final moments. It took a hold of her, taking her to a place where she never wanted to go.

Sarah pulled back. She couldn't do it. She emptied the chest instead and, with some effort, stuffed the Hex inside. She piled another chest and several bags filled with grain and potatoes overtop. The old witch wouldn't be getting out any time soon.

A faint thumping came from a different chest in the corner. A familiar aura touched her senses. It was alive, whatever or whoever it was. Sarah's fear and anger must have prevented her from detecting it when she first entered.

The present the Hex was talking about. Oh my gods, another child! She ran to the chest and skidded to her knees. She fumbled with the metal clasps until the lid swung open.

Sarah knelt there, frozen on the spot. A girl lay curled in the cramped trunk, bound and gagged, with a heavy bruise stretching across her white-blond hairline. It took precious seconds for Sarah's brain to register who she saw.

"Brenna?"

Sarah quickly undid the young witch's bonds and pulled the gag from her mouth.

"She… she t-took me," the girl bawled. "She took me right out of my room."

Sarah helped Brenna out of the trunk. She was wearing a nightgown. Bruises covered her arms and legs. "Who took you? How did you get caught? Where's Grayle?"

"What? Who?" Brenna's eyelids fluttered, tears streaked down her face.

"Grayle. You were with him in the town square."

"I don't know what you're talking about," she cried. "She came to Midgard last night. She shapeshifted and took me!"

"Who?"

"Hel! She came, and I couldn't stop her." Brenna buried her face in Sarah's shoulder, sobbing uncontrollably.

"But if you were taken from Midgard, then who's with…" Sarah's eyes widened.

Grayle.

They needed to find him—fast.

Chapter 31

The mob gathering in Baldersted's square swirled around Grayle in an overlapping mass of heads, cloaks, and arms. The confusion made it easier to stay unnoticed but harder to keep an eye on those he was hiding from. To make matters worse, Mussels was nowhere in sight. Grayle moved along the alcoves and shops lining the square, perfect for ducking into just in case the bodyguard decided to double back.

Brenna followed close behind.

Almost too close.

More than once, Grayle thought he could feel her breathing down his neck.

"Give me some room, will ya," he said, stopping in a niche outside a butcher's shop. He ignored her angry glare and scanned the plaza.

Still no Mussels.

"We can't free the old lady and play hide-and-seek at the

same time," he said. "I need you to find and distract the body-guard while I try to free her."

Brenna shifted her balance and crossed her arms.

"Don't worry. He doesn't know you," Grayle reasoned. "All you have to do is—"

"I'll think of something," she snapped. "How are *you* going to get close enough to the woman's cage with all these people around?"

Between the size of the platform and the space taken up by the market stalls, nearly three hundred people were packed tight into square.

Definitely not enough seclusion to spring a suspected witch from her cell, Grayle thought. *If only I could become completely invisible, not just in front of cameras, then I might have a chance.*

But he had nothing—no powers, no super strength or spells that could help him.

"I'll think of something too," he said. "Good luck."

Brenna retreated into the crowd, elbowing her way to the far side of the square. Grayle watched her continue her search for Mussels there, all the while keeping one eye fixed on him. Clearly, she still didn't trust him when their only focus should be on saving the woman.

And how exactly am I going to do that?

Grayle stood by helplessly as four guards struggled to lift the heavy cage with the woman inside and, with a loud clang, set it down beside the raised platform. The woman was yanked out and hauled up the stairs, shrieking, "I'm not the Hex—can't you see that?" The guards ignored her pleas, tying her hands securely to the scorched tree.

Grayle shuddered, wondering how many people had been tied to it and burned alive.

The bell gonged inside the clock tower.

Noon.

Grayle racked his brain for a plan. *What can I do? There are too many people and not enough time to—*

He spied Mussels standing in the shadows of the pretzel stand off to his right. Brenna spotted him too. She slinked toward him. The bodyguard didn't pay her any attention. All he would see was a blond girl, nothing to do with the witch he was searching for. But as Brenna came closer, the man instinctively reached for something under his cloak.

Grayle panicked. *Is he reaching for a gun?*

Cheers erupted. People's heads and bodies blocked Grayle's view before he could see what happened next. He craned his neck, but it was no use. The crowd pushed, forcing him closer to the platform. He searched frantically in Brenna's direction. The blond witch was gone. So was Mussels.

A fat man approached the stage. As wide as he was tall, he made Mrs. Zito look like a runway model. He wore the same chain mail as the other guards, but the metal links were almost coming undone from the pressure of his enormous belly. A black hood covered the top of the man's face, leaving only his eyes, mouth, and stubbly double chins exposed. Grayle had read about hooded figures like this in his history books. The man was an executioner, someone who carried out death sentences ordered by the local legal authority—in this case, whoever ruled Baldersted.

The executioner used a pike with a curved axe-blade at its tip to support his bulk up the platform's steps. The steps strained underneath his weight. He strode to the platform's edge and pounded the end of his pike on the wooden planks, knocking repeatedly until the crowd grew silent. He straightened and rested a bloated fist on his hip. "Now behold the awful crime of witchcraft," he announced for all to hear.

More cheers and heckles bursted from the crowd.

"Burn the witch!" someone shouted.

"We want justice!" yelled another voice farther away.

The mob surged forward. Some threw bushels of hay at the structure's base, chanting, "Burn the witch! Burn the witch! Burn the witch!"

An absurd amount of kindling began to accumulate, enough to burn ten witches.

"Is there anyone here who disputes the allegations?" the executioner called out, daring anyone to answer. His question was met with sporadic laughter and boos.

This whole thing is a sham. But Grayle couldn't bring himself to say anything in the woman's defense. He wasn't sure which he hated more, his own cowardice or how the man under the hood revelled in the mob's cruelty.

"Very well," the executioner said, facing the sobbing woman. "You are sentenced to burn at the stake for witchcraft and murder. Do you have anything to say?"

Wearily, the old woman lifted her head. "It's not me!" she cried out one last time.

"Of course it isn't," the executioner agreed, but his voice held no sympathy. "Let the punishment commence!" He spun on his heels and followed the guards off the platform.

A roar of approval rose from the gathered onlookers.

Seven couples dressed in black robes stepped forward, each brandishing torches.

Parents of the missing children, Grayle guessed.

A torch dropped then another and another, until the kindling ignited.

They're going to do it—they're going to burn her alive!

He looked to his left and right but saw only half-crazed faces.

The flames spread quickly, burning through the dry straw and reaching the platform's support posts. The crowd went ballistic.

Grayle pushed his way closer to the platform. He had to reach her. Even if it meant exposing himself as a sympathizer and getting caught, he couldn't stand by and let this happen.

A horn pierced the mob's whoops and howls. The cheers muted, and silence followed, except for the crackling flames still eating away at the platform. The horn blared again, more urgently this time. Soldiers unsheathed their swords, reacting to some unseen threat with trained readiness.

A boy came running into the square. "Frost Giants! Frost Giants are coming!" he shouted. "Frost Giants are—"

His words were cut off by a concentrated torrent of ice and snow streaming from somewhere behind the adjacent buildings. The ice swirled like a cyclone, smothering the boy and instantly encasing him in ice.

The crowd gaped in shock.

Then all chaos broke loose.

Two Jotun, nearly as tall as the surrounding buildings, thundered into the plaza, one swinging an axe, the other a club the size of a tree trunk. Both had reindeer skins and polar bear hides wrapped around their torsos. Dented shields, fashioned into armor plates, overlapped their grey chests and shoulders like dragon scales.

"Find him," ordered the first giant. He had a white beard and wore the horned skull of an animal on his head. He seemed to be the one in charge.

Grayle was knocked around like a pinball as the crowd scattered, screaming in mass panic, fleeing for their lives.

"How do we know he's here?" the second Jotun growled over the commotion.

"He's got to be here. The Outlander said so."

With icicles jingling in his blue beard, the second Frost Giant breathed in deeply. "Yes, I smell him, Thrym, but I cannot isolate him. Blasted fire!" He coughed, snorting smoke from the burning platform.

Columns of Baldersted guards took positions in the square, forming two lines in front of the giants. They raised their pikes and drew their bows.

The Jotun seemed indifferent, continuing to smash stalls and toss carts aside.

"Ready!" one guard shouted. "Fire!"

A volley of arrows sliced the air. Some missed the giants, some bounced harmlessly off their plated armor, but a few punctured their grey flesh.

"Filthy humans." Thrym pulled out an arrow as if it were a toothpick. "Freeze everyone, Bergelmir," he yelled, swiping his axe in a wide arc and mowing down several soldiers. "We'll sniff him out after."

The blue-bearded Frost Giant levelled his club at the remaining troops. With the howl of a thousand snowstorms, another blizzard shot from his weapon.

Grayle crouched, staring open-mouthed. The soldiers had been frozen in mid-attack. His shock was interrupted by an ear-splitting scream.

The old woman.

He could see her through the heat distortion, eyes shut and lips moving in silent prayer. How was he going to get to her? The platform was too high and already half engulfed in flames.

He clenched his teeth and wrestled a pike away from one of the frozen guards. He held the weapon in his hands. It felt heavy, almost two and a half times his body length. He backed away several paces and, drawing from his training in Gloomshroud, rushed forward. After gaining enough speed, Grayle drove the spear's tip between two cobblestones. The shaft bent into a taut *C* and lifted him over the fire. He felt the wash of heat below him before landing hard on the platform.

"That's going to leave a mark." He grimaced and quickly picked himself up.

The heat was excruciating. Smoke stung his eyes, making it difficult to see or breathe. Flames poked through the floorboards, the planks too hot to touch. Grayle was afraid they'd give way at any moment, plunging him into the growing inferno below. He covered his nose and mouth with his cloak and stumbled to where the woman hung by her tied arms, barely conscious.

Using the dagger he'd stolen from Lothar, Grayle cut her free and dragged her to the platform's edge. He lifted the woman high enough to keep her flimsy clothes from catching fire.

Now what, genius?

There was no way to douse the flames or jump off without searing them both into well-done steaks.

This can't be how it ends.

He needed to find the Eye of Odin and learn about his past. He needed to know he was more than an orphan, more than just a thief. He needed to be someone different, so different that…

Sarah's words rang in his ears: "Magic doesn't affect you."

I need to be someone who can't be affected by magic.

A plan began to take shape, a plan that would kill him if he was wrong. But with time running out, he couldn't see any other way.

"Hey, you! Frost Giant! I'm over here!"

Both Thrym and Bergelmir stopped their bashing and looked his way.

Bergelmir breathed in deeply. "It's him." He grunted and plodded toward the platform. He halted a few yards away, the heat keeping him at a distance.

No surprise that fire would be a Frost Giant's weakness. "What are you waiting for?" Grayle shouted. "Too stupid to use your club?"

Bergelmir snarled, stalking the burning platform like a caged lion searching for a way to get at his prey.

C'mon... use the club, Grayle begged. His eyes watered. Breathing became all but impossible. Charred and in flames, the boards beneath his feet began to snap.

The giant lifted his weapon.

Even though Grayle knew what was coming, it took all his courage to keep from jumping aside as the snowstorm shot toward him. He sheltered the woman's body with his own. Cold exploded around them like a thousand air conditioners at full blast. But the ice never latched on, freezing everything in Grayle's wake until the entire wooden structure resembled a land-locked iceberg.

The fire had extinguished without as much as a hiss.

Still holding the woman in his arms, Grayle slid down the ice, over the platform's edge, and onto the cobblestoned square. He lowered her gently to the ground. She was unconscious, her legs white and frostbitten. Her breathing was shallow and her face grimy from heat and smoke, but she was alive.

"All right, lady, you're on your own," he said, taking off his cloak and spreading it over her. He'd done the best he could. Staying with her would only put her in more danger.

"You're coming with us, runt," Bergelmir bellowed, rounding the frozen platform.

"Not today," Grayle said and bolted for the nearest side street. He felt the tremors of footsteps behind him as the giants gave chase.

"You can't escape, anklebiter," one of them shouted.

An arctic blast exploded to Grayle's right, smothering a nearby cart in inches of ice.

How long until they figure out their magic can't freeze me?

He tore down another street, pumping his arms and legs even faster.

Thrym and Bergelmir's steps faltered. Their size kept them from making the sharp corner. They recovered quickly and started to gain on him.

Brenna emerged from an alcove ahead.

"Run!" Grayle shouted, flapping his hands as if shooing her away.

"This way!" she hollered, motioning for him to hurry. She pointed into an alley.

Grayle scuttled inside, but the girl never followed.

"Now!" he heard her shout.

Grayle looked back long enough to see Bergelmir lift his club, trying to get a fix on him as he shimmied through the alleyway. Ice sheared down the corridor, nipping at his heels. Grayle knew he wouldn't freeze, but in this confined space, everything around him would, trapping him in ice like some woolly mammoth. The alley narrowed. Frost crawled on either side, beginning to overtake him. Grayle jumped, tumbling out onto the adjacent street just as ice plugged the alley shut.

Grayle shot to his feet again, only to be bulled over by the jester he'd seen in the square earlier. Their collision sent them sprawling. The man's juggling pins clattered along the cobblestones.

"Head for the docks, boy," the jester wheezed, helping Grayle up and steadying him. "Find a ship. It's your only cha—" His breath suddenly hitched and his body went slack. Grayle caught the man and laid him on the ground. A feathered dart stuck out of his back.

"What the—"

Something zinged past Grayle's shoulder. He looked up to see Mussels standing forty feet away.

He was aiming a crossbow.

Reacting on instinct, Grayle left the jester on the road and dove into an abandoned stall. He fell over a counter and flattened himself behind it.

"Come out, Hexhunter!" Mussels shouted.

For a moment, Grayle thought the bodyguard was talking to someone else. He risked a peek over the counter to be sure.

Big mistake.

Another dart whistled by. Its tail feathers brushed his cheek and dug into a wooden table behind him.

Grayle crouched back down, thinking what to do next.

I can't stay here. I'm like a duck in a shooting gallery.

He heard a faint click. The bodyguard was reloading his crossbow.

Grayle scurried from his hiding place and shot out from the stall. He didn't get far. The bodyguard had moved within ten yards of his position. Dropping the crossbow, Mussels clotheslined him with a single arm and expertly kicked his legs out from under him.

Grayle hit the cobblestones.

The Brawler knelt down and pressed a knee into his sternum. "You're not going anywhere," he growled, grabbing a fistful of Grayle's hair. "Monsieur Caine wants to take you alive, but you and your witch girlfriend are… how do you say? *Trop de difficultés*—too much trouble? If there was only some way to get rid of you." A thought seemed to dawn on the bodyguard. Grayle could see it flicker then take hold in his beady eyes. "I can make it look like an accident. Oui… perhaps you fell and broke your neck." His gorilla-sized hands clutched Grayle's head on each side. "One simple twist and the Inquisition need not concern itself with you any longer."

Two shadows stretched over the road before Mussels could follow through on his threat. Thrym and Bergelmir came lumbering into the square.

"Away, anklebiter!" Thrym rumbled, ready to smack Mussels aside. "You have no business claiming our prize."

"*My* prize." Brenna called out, appearing behind the Frost Giant's trunk-like legs. As she came closer, her white-blond hair darkened to strands of yellow. She grew several inches taller, her tunic swelled into a shadowy cloak, and her face melted away, revealing Hel's half-decayed form.

"The boy is mine… as we agreed, Jotun," she said, keeping her menacing gaze on Grayle. "He will make an excellent slave."

As if on cue, a draugr—like one from Grayle's nightmares—materialized in a swath of smoke and brimstone next to her.

Grayle's heart thumped. *There's no way I'm becoming a zombie.* He writhed and kicked under Mussels' weight like a salmon trapped beneath a grizzly's paw. He clawed at the ground, fingernails scratching the cold stone until they wrapped around one of the jester's juggling pins. Grayle swung the pin like a club, bashing the rounded end into Mussels's skull. Stunned, the bodyguard's weight shifted enough for Grayle to wriggle out from under him. He scrambled to his feet and bolted.

"Stop him, Bergelmir!" Hel screeched.

A column of sleet and snow arched over Grayle before he could exit the square. It solidified into a wall of ice, growing high to the rooftops and spanning the width of the street.

"Now freeze him," Hel ordered.

Bergelmir let slip a gap-toothed grin and aimed his club.

Grayle shut his eyes. Like on the platform, a concentrated wave blasted his body. Ice snapped and cracked as layers formed around him. When he opened his eyes, Grayle saw he'd been encased in an icy cocoon with barely enough room to move. He reached up, running a palm over the smooth surface. It was thick and solid, like an igloo without a door. He pounded against the ice to no effect. He stepped back and threw himself at it. Pain shot through his arm, but the ice never cracked.

Through the faint translucence, he detected Hel's silhouette approaching. She rested a metal gauntlet on the outside wall.

"What now, goddess?" asked Thrym. Grayle could barely make out the Frost Giant's voice.

"We wait for the cold to render him unconscious," she answered. "Then I will take him to Helheim."

Chapter 32

Grayle sat curled in a ball, trying to stay warm. Every inch of his body shook. Within half a minute of being confined to his refrigerator prison, the cold had numbed his nose, ears, fingers, and toes. A full minute after that, it had penetrated his tunic, biting at his skin. He might be impervious to Bergelmir's blizzard wielding club, but he wasn't immune to its subzero temperatures.

"Exactly what Hel was counting on," he mumbled miserably to himself. "I'll be going to hell as a Grayle-sicle."

His depressed laugh came out in misty puffs.

When did the goddess take on Brenna's form? When I lost sight of her in the square? Before then? He shook his head. *The real question is "What does she want with me?" Odin mentioned I was important, but important how? And Mussels said Caine wants me alive. There has to be a reason.*

Too distracted thinking about his impending doom, he never

noticed the jagged cracks snapping and breaking along the wall behind him. It wasn't until steam started filling the confined space that he turned clumsily and faced the opposite wall. A bright light appeared on the other side, growing larger and more intense. Grayle thought he heard voices too—and not those of Hel and the giants. They were coming from elsewhere, muffled and distorted.

"Careful or you'll bring the whole wall down on him."

"I know what I'm doing."

The ice melted until a gaping hole steamed in front of him. A pair of hands reached in and pulled him out.

"Thank Odin you're alright," Sarah whispered, hugging him.

Grayle's legs were so frozen he could hardly stand, but the warmth of Sarah's embrace, the reassurance of her touch, steadied him. He glanced over her shoulder. Lothar was there, somehow looking both nervous and unimpressed at the same time. Grayle tensed when he saw Brenna.

He began to stammer, "S-she's not—"

"Easy," Sarah said, calming him. "We know what happened. This is the real Brenna." She took off her cloak and fastened it securely around his neck. "C'mon. We have to get out of here." She scanned the ice wall. "I don't want to be around when Hel finds you gone."

"Quick. To the water," Lothar urged. "I can conjure a bifrost there."

They ran down a long avenue, passing empty buildings with windows and doors left wide open. People's belongings lay strewn across the street, abandoned during their exodus from the city.

It took several strides for Grayle to find his legs again. The cold gave way to a tingling, pins-and-needles warmth. "How did you find me?" he asked, doing his best to keep up.

Sarah slowed to match his pace. "Wasn't that hard. We went back to where we left you, saw a gigantic wall of ice, and noticed a snow globe bulge at its base. Didn't take a genius to figure out you were inside."

"And where did you find Brenna… the real Brenna?"

The blond witch ran in barefeet ten yards ahead of them, sidestepping a broken chair left on the street.

"In the Hex's lair. She was taken last night, before we even entered the bifrost."

Grayle remembered his dream, how he'd been in Hel's head as she weaved through Midgard's corridors. She had stopped in front of a door. He couldn't have known it was the door to Brenna's room at the time.

"If I'm supposed to be impervious to magic, why wasn't I able to see through Hel's disguise?"

"Your *body* is impervious to magical attack," Sarah explained, "but it seems your senses can be fooled—just like mine. I didn't notice a change in her aura either."

"If Hel's been with us since this morning, that means she knows our plans."

Sarah nodded. "And now it looks like she's working with Caine."

They arrived at Baldersted's harbor. This part of the city extended out over the fjord's frozen shores. Great wooden beams supported houses and shops built along the docks. Two large pulleys acting as medieval cranes towered at the edge of the dock, ready to load and unload cargo. Barrels and crates were stacked high, ready for export to who-knows-where. Grayle noticed some were marked with large X's in red paint.

Over thirty ships had weighed anchor in the fjord. With their walls breached and city compromised, the people of Baldersted had sought refuge on the open water.

Smart thinking, Grayle thought as he followed Lothar, Brenna, and Sarah down one of two piers extending into the fjord. Their feet tromped on the wooden boards. Sheets of surface ice checkered the water below them like a chessboard.

"Start conjuring!" Sarah told Lothar once they reached the pier's far edge.

For once, the prince didn't argue. He shut his eyes, spread his arms toward the water, and chanted the spell. Sweat dripped from his scalp. His words stuttered.

Nothing happened.

Sarah took Lothar's hand. The blue glow of her magic spread from her body to his.

Grayle felt a pang of jealousy, but whatever they were doing seemed to work.

Mist gathered over the water. The ice cracked and the faint swirl of a whirlpool appeared. As the funnel intensified, an image of Midgard materialized at its center. When the portal reached its maximum aperture, the bifrost's rainbow shot from its depths and arched high into the stratosphere.

Lothar pulled his hand free of Sarah's. "Come… make haste. We'll take the Hex's information straight to my father." He turned to jump into the bifrost.

"Wait!" Sarah said. "You forgot something."

"What?"

She clenched a fist and punched him hard in the nose.

Brenna gasped. "Sarah! What are you—?"

"That's for betraying Grayle," she said.

The prince whimpered. Blood leaked from his nostrils. "He's a Hexhunter, Sarah! Do you think my father or anyone else will let him live beyond his usefulness?"

"And this," she went on, "is for being such an ass." She lifted a leg and front kicked him in the chest.

Arms flailing, Lothar toppled off the pier and disappeared into the bifrost.

Brenna winced. "You're going to be in *so* much trouble when we—"

"What was he talking about?" Grayle cut in. "What's a Hexhunter?" It was the second time he'd heard that word and both times were in reference to him.

Sarah shook her hand. "I'll tell you as soon as we get out of here."

"Then let's go." He held out his arms, waiting for her to see him safely through the portal.

"We're not going back."

"What? Are you crazy?"

"There's still a traitor in Midgard, Grayle. How else was Hel able to get into the city and take Brenna? Beings from the other Nine Realms shouldn't be able to get in, not without help—not without magical help. Whoever did must still be *in* Midgard. It's not safe."

"Then I don't want to go back either," Brenna said.

"Hel won't be coming after you. She wants Grayle and the runestones, not you."

"Why does she want me?"

Sarah ignored him. "You have to go, Brenna. You have to go now."

"But I want to help."

"You can help by exposing the traitor in Midgard."

She relented. "Fine. But before I go, you need to know what the Hex told the big man, the one who brought me here this morning. I overheard her say something about a capital in the east…"

Sarah eased Brenna to the edge of the dock. "I already know," she said impatiently. "You need to—"

"And there was something else. She used a word—a word I've never heard before. *Var… varange… Varangians*, that's it. *Varangians*."

Sarah grabbed her gently by the shoulders. "You're sure? *Varangians*… the Hex said *Varangians*?"

Brenna nodded.

"Does that mean anything to you?" Grayle asked.

Sarah's eyes darted back and forth as though she were connecting dots in her mind. "It might." She pressed something into Brenna's hand. "Find your father. Tell him everything that's happened, no one else. Not even Loremaster Onem. Once you've discovered the traitor's identity, come find us. Understand?"

Brenna nodded and turned to face the bifrost. "Good luck," she said then jumped into the mist. The rainbow fluctuated as her body catapulted skyward.

Grayle watched the magical gateway fade away, their only chance at escape along with it. They were stranded near the Arctic Circle, in a town overrun by giants, and not a single ship remained in the harbor, not even a rowboat.

"So how are *we* going to get out of here?" he asked.

Bergelmir burst onto the waterfront before Sarah could answer. The giant bled from several arrows sticking out of his arms and legs. Apparently he and the others had more run-ins with Baldersted's soldiers. The giant sniffed the air like a wild dog. "Found you, anklebiter!" he shouted, spotting them at the end of the pier.

"We're in big trouble," Sarah warned.

Bergelmir plodded toward them, smacking his club ominously in his palm. Thrym and five more giants came thundering down the avenue behind him.

"Not big trouble," Grayle said, swallowing hard. "Giant trouble."

Chapter 33

Sarah regretted not taking the bifrost when she and Grayle had the chance. Seeing Bergelmir storming toward them was enough to send any witch running. Problem was, stuck at the edge of the pier, there was no place left *to* run.

Bergelmir went to step onto the pier. The wooden planks snapped and broke under his weight. He stopped and stepped back off.

"Looks like you won't be able to get me after all," Grayle taunted.

The Frost Giant's face contorted into a snarl. He straddled the pier and lifted his club.

Sarah groaned. "You just had to say something, didn't you."

The club came down, crushing the dock's supports. A shockwave rippled down the length of the pier, throwing Sarah and Grayle off their feet.

"Stop!" Thrym shouted. He and five other Jotun plodded onto the docks. "We need him alive!"

Bergelmir ignored his leader's orders, repeatedly bashing the pier like a four-year-old playing whack-a-mole—without the mole.

The pier buckled, rocking violently as though an earthquake was twisting it apart. Sarah scrambled to hold onto the wooden boards. The world turned sideways. The next thing she knew, she was in the water. Her senses screamed. The cold assaulted her body. When she surfaced, she found Grayle floundering beside her, spitting water and gasping for air.

Bergelmir jumped into the fjord, charging after them in a burst of whitewater and icy debris. His club teetered high over his head, ready to bash them like fish in a barrel. Whether from fear or the water's mind-numbing chill, Sarah was powerless to move. But the waves from the giant's wake pushed them up and out of range just as the club crashed into the water with a thundering whoosh.

Bergelmir roared in frustration. He waded deeper, readying his club for another wallop when a crack sounded. Something ripped into his shoulder, spattering blue blood behind him.

"Keep swimmin', you varmints!" Grigsby shouted over the chaos. The elf had one boot hoisted on the *Drakkar's* railing, aiming his Winchester. The weapon fired again, but Sarah didn't see whether Grigsby hit his mark or not. She was too busy keeping her arms stroking and legs kicking, heading for the longship as it cut through the ice toward her. The shield strapped to her back impeded her progress. She slid it off and, with the last of her magic, willed it to triple in size. The shield's convex shape bobbed in the water like a life raft.

Sarah pulled herself inside and turned, expecting Grayle to be floating nearby. But between the rolling waves and overturned ice, she couldn't see him anywhere.

"Here!" Grigs shouted, reaching out to take her hand.

Sarah barely had enough strength to lift her arm.

He snatched her sleeve and hoisted her and the shield aboard.

"Where's the prince and Brenna?" Grigsby asked, propping Sarah on her feet.

"No time... to explain," she said between heavy breaths.

She stumbled to the railing, desperately scanning the water for Grayle. She spotted him halfway between the ship and the docks. Arms thrashing, he struggled to keep his head above water. Then he disappeared under the ice.

No!

She went to jump in after him.

"No, Sarah." Grigsby wrapped an arm around her waist.

"But he'll drown."

"So will you. You'll never survive if you go back in."

He was right. The water had nearly paralyzed her muscles, sucked the energy from her body. And having exhausted her magic, she'd never be able to get herself and Grayle back to the ship. But letting him drown wasn't an option either.

I brought him into this. If he dies—

Arrows suddenly arched past the *Drakkar's* stern, thwishing by in a mass of mini-missiles. They rained down on the Frost Giants gathered at the docks, piercing their armor and skin. Some arrows fell short, plunging into the water where Grayle had vanished moments ago.

Sarah tore away from Grigsby and ran across the deck. Rows of archers had gathered along the starboard sides of each Balderstedian ship. They strung new arrows and prepared to fire again.

"Stop!" she shouted. "There's still someone in the water. Stop!"

Whether they ignored her on purpose or couldn't hear her above the splashing waves, another volley of arrows let loose.

Sarah waved her arms. "Stop. There's someone in—"

Her voice trailed off, recognizing a large crossbow-like weapon mounted on the bow of the nearest ship. A ballista—a machine designed to fire three meter long arrows with iron tips the size of her forearm. All Sarah could do was stare as soldiers cranked a winch wheel, stretching the ballista's bowstring to maximum tautness. A massive arrow was placed into a wooden slider next, then lit on fire.

The ballista swivelled in their direction.

"Drakkar. Hard to port!" Sarah shouted.

The ship steered left, responding sluggishly against the ice battering its hull.

Grigsby rushed to the rudder and shoved his weight against it.

The flaming arrow launched. It narrowly missed the *Drakkar's* mainsail and struck the crates marked with X's on the docks. The crates billowed outwards in fiery balls of orange flame. Shrapnel blasted into nearby giants with devastating effect, tearing through their armor, and lodging deep into their faces, arms, and legs.

The people crowding the ships cheered.

Sarah realized they'd had a plan to deal with invading Frost Giants all along: escape to a place of safety, draw the giants to a confined area, then counterattack. The crates had been filled with explosives and loose debris, planted there on purpose just for this kind of occasion.

It was these people who helped the Inquisition round up magickers and creatures of the Mythic Races centuries ago. It was these people who had participated in the Great Purge. They were prepared to defeat their enemies at all costs, even willing to sacrifice their own city in order to get the job done.

Sarah both feared and respected their tenacity.

She returned her focus to the water.

How long has Grayle been under? A minute? Longer?

More agonizing seconds passed.

No one could survive the frigid waters for much longer.

No one.

Chapter 34

The frigid waters crippled Grayle's muscles. His legs felt like lead weights. His arms slapped the surface in a vain attempt to stay afloat. Worse, the cloak Sarah had given him had become so waterlogged, the extra weight was dragging him under. He took one last panicked breath before slipping beneath the waves. The cold stung his face. Rays of daylight seeping among the ice sheets grew dimmer as the cloak pulled him deeper. His numb fingers fumbled for the dagger in his belt. He managed to pull it out and slice through the cloak's material. He tugged it off, losing the knife in the process.

Lungs burning, Grayle fought to resurface. What air he had left bubbled from his nose and mouth. An ice slab blocked his ascent. Inches separated him from precious oxygen. He pushed against the slab, but it refused to budge.

Zip. Thunk. Zip. Zip. Thunk.

Arrows sliced into the water and punctured the ice sheet above him. An arrowhead stopped a hair short of taking out his eye. Grayle didn't have time to thank his luck. Grabbing the arrow shafts, he pulled himself along the slab's underside. His fingers groped until he found the edge. With his last ounce of strength, he squeezed between two ice sheets and broke through to the surface.

Grayle gasped for breath. His chest heaved until he regained his senses.

He surveyed the scene around him.

Arrows stuck to the surrounding ice like pin cushions. Smoke and fire consumed the docks. A charred crater smouldered where shipping crates had been stacked. Dead Frost Giants lay in the burning rubble. The others, including Thrym and Bergelmir, were in full retreat, dragging their wounded comrades from the harbor.

A rope ladder splashed to Grayle's right.

"Grab hold!" Sarah shouted.

His hands were like frozen claws. All he could do was hook an arm through the lowest rung and let himself be dragged to the longship.

Sarah and Grigsby pulled him aboard. He staggered on deck, shivering uncontrollably.

"Set a course for Istanbul," Sarah yelled.

The *Drakkar*'s sail billowed, catching a magical gust.

Grigsby returned aft to man the rudder.

"Istanbul! What m-makes you th-think the next c-c-clue's there?" Grayle asked. He braced himself against the mast as the ship veered from Baldersted's harbor.

"I'll explain when we get there. We can reach the city by this afternoon."

"Hel can d-disappear and move like the wind! While we're w-wasting time on this glorified f-ferry—"

The *Drakkar* groaned in protest.

"S-sorry," Grayle called out, "but Hel and Caine are going to get there f-first. They'll find the runestones, maybe even the Eye, and then…" He was about to say, *then I won't be able to use it to find my parents.*

Sarah huffed. "Good luck with that. They'll have little chance of finding it without y—" She stopped abruptly, staring at him with an I-can't-believe-I-just-said-that look.

"Without… what? Me?" Grayle asked. "They can't find the Eye without me?"

She pursed her lips and rubbed her hands nervously on her thighs.

"What makes *me* so important?" Grayle pressed. "What do you know about me that I don't?

She opened her mouth, but hesitated to say more.

"Sarah, you *have* to tell me."

She exhaled and bit her lip. "No matter what I say, promise me you'll keep helping me."

"But I don't even—"

"Promise me! And not just to find the next runestone," she added. "Until the very end—until this mission is over."

"We'll probably be dead by then."

Sarah shook her head. "Hel and Caine need you alive."

"You should m-mention that to Mussels," Grayle shot back, recalling the bodyguard's hands ready to twist his head off like a bottle cap. Then again, the bodyguard had said Caine wanted him alive and Hel took on Brenna's form to get close to him. She could've killed him at any time, but she didn't.

What Grayle still didn't know was why.

"Why am I so important? Why do they need me alive?"

Sarah squared her shoulders. Her next words came out slow

as if they could inflict pain. "Because you're a Hexhunter," she said.

Grayle had figured out that much for himself. "So? What does it mean?"

"It's too much to get into—"

"No. T-tell me now. What's a Hexhunter?"

She let out another long sigh. "Hexhunters were once Folklore's most dangerous enemies. They hunted down witches and carried out assassinations, murdering thousands. They were said to have skills and powers—one of them being impervious to magic, like you, and apparently they're also drawn to all things magic including—"

"Magical artifacts," Grayle whispered.

The ship went silent, except for the splashing waves and ice knocking against the hull.

Grayle let his back slide down the mast. "How long have you known?" he asked. "How long have you known I was a Hexhunter?"

"I've suspected for a while," she said, averting her eyes from his.

A while? She's known for a while and never told me?

Grayle should have felt angry, betrayed—and he did—but he also felt an odd sense of relief. Being a Hexhunter may explain his weirdness, why he wasn't able to be photographed or why the runestone reacted to his proximity back in the Vancouver Museum. But with this new information came new questions.

"How many Hexhunters are there?" he asked. "Where do I—they—come from?"

"You're the first Hexhunter in three hundred years," Sarah said. "As for where you came from…" She paused and looked out onto the fjord. A fog, like the magical barrier protecting

Midgard, enveloped the ship. "I think there's a good chance you came from one of the Kingdoms of Folklore."

"A good chance. Can't you tell? Can't you see my aura?"

"No. I can't."

"You were able to spot Zito as a Folklorian easily enough."

"You don't understand. Hexhunters are impervious to magic and..."

"And what?"

"They don't have auras. *You* don't have an aura."

"So what does *that* mean?" He remembered Sarah describing auras as being the luminous energies that surrounded all living things. If he didn't have an aura then...

He swallowed. "Am I... am I dead? Am I some kind of draugr?"

Sarah tried to hide a smile. "No. You're very much alive, just... different." She knelt down and brought her face closer to his. She cupped his cheeks in her palms.

His teeth stopped chattering.

"Listen to me," she said softly. "I need you, not because of your skills, not because without you the world is doomed, but because I..." she hesitated, "because you're my friend. Got it?"

Grayle didn't know what to say. He had spent years relying solely on himself, dreaming of a time when a person or family would be there to help him, to protect him. He couldn't believe Sarah was willing to be that person, especially when she knew he was a Hexhunter—a witch's worst enemy.

She was willing to do that... *except tell me the truth,* he reminded himself. *Who knows what other secrets she's keeping from me?*

He looked at her. Frost had built on the tips of her hair and the color had washed from her face. But her eyes—those blue eyes—they reached into him, trying to melt away whatever doubts he had about her.

"Promise you'll help," she said again. "If we work together, we have a good chance of finding the runestones—maybe even the Eye. I need to hear you say it."

The magnitude of their situation—and his role in it—became clear. The world—mankind's very survival—was at stake.

But he wasn't going to tell her the other reason he wanted the Eye. He knew she was smart enough to suspect it, but as long as he withheld the information, it was a topic they didn't need to face.

For now.

"I promise I'll help you," he said finally, putting on a brave face.

Chapter 35

The Operative watched the mayhem from a ridge overlooking the city. A symphony of chaos and destruction echoed below. Baldersted's walls had been breached in multiple places. Jotun had poured in, bashing through the streets and alleyways. Smoke billowed from where fires had broken out, some set deliberately to allow townspeople time to escape, others ignited during skirmishes with the grey-skinned giants. All the while, a choir of helpless screaming came from those still trapped in the carnage.

The Operative tossed his jester's mask in the snow, relieved to be rid of it. He pulled on a black toque in its place. It slipped on easily, fitting loosely around the empty space where ears should have been.

An explosion rocked the city's docks. The Operative looked up in time to see giants being thrown off their feet, tossed aside like toy puppets by the blast wave. A rising mushroom cloud darkened the sky and the hoarse howls of injured Jotun added to the symphony.

Impressive, the Operative thought. In one swift counterattack, the Baldersted soldiers had turned the tide of the battle. The Frost Giants were retreating, leaving the town and their casualties behind.

He scanned the fjord.

The Viking ship had joined a jumble of bright-colored sails fleeing the city.

The witch and boy had made it out safely.

Their safety, however, was not the Operative's primary concern. If that were the case, he would have done more than shield the boy when Mussels tried to shoot him with the crossbow. He reached behind him, feeling where the dart had pierced his Kevlar vest beneath the jester costume. The tranquilizer had failed to penetrate his skin, but the Operative faked unconsciousness all the same. There was little even he could do against two giants and a goddess.

He pulled his cell phone from beneath his cloak and dialled.

A woman answered this time. "Operative, what do you have to report?"

East Indian, the Operative assumed, according to the accent.

"The Hexhunter and witch are on the move again," he said.

"With the information they needed?" The voice was level and as emotionless as a robot.

"Affirmative."

"Good. Do you know the location of the next runestone?"

"No, ma'am. But I will shortly." He switched to a tracking app on his phone. It followed the tracing beacon he'd slipped into the Hexhunter's tunic during their collision. The device was no larger than a grain of rice.

"Very well. Maintain your surveillance and keep us informed. Remember, there is no margin for error."

The phone connection ended.

The Operative scanned the horizon, spotting the longship before it disappeared in a fog bank. Then he returned his focus to the red blip winking across his phone screen.

Wherever the Hexhunter and witch were going, he would follow. It would only be a matter of time before his surveillance orders switched to kill orders.

He smiled, knowing that when that time came—kids or not—he'd be hanging more ears from people's necks.

Acknowledgments

First, I would like to acknowledge YOU, yes... YOU, dear reader, for finishing this book and finding the time to read these acknowledgments. Let's face it, we usually skip this part. I'd like to tell you there's not about to be a list of names of people you don't know, but I'd be lying. Without these individuals, this book would not have been possible.

So here we go.

To Steven Whibley, for his ongoing advice during my road to publication. To Ian and Patricia Robertson, Luke Corrigan and Christine McCauley, for their belief and enthusiasm in this project. To Pintado, for an amazing cover. To Jennifer Pendergast, for her illustrations of Mimir's Stone (more pieces to come). To the editorial staff at Red Adept Publishing, especially Michelle and Kelly—their efforts turned this book from a crude stone to a polished gem. To J.R.R. Tolkien, whose Sindarin Elvish language forms the basis of Sarah's magical incantations. To Steven Spielberg (yes, *that* Steven Spielberg), for bringing Jurassic Park to the big screen and turning a young, non-reader like me to Michael Crichton. To my parents, Udo and Kirsten, who let their dreamy kid live inside his head when there were probably chores to be done. And last but not least, to my wife, Shannon, for your patience and support during this journey.

About the Author

Dennis Staginnus dreamed of becoming an archaeologist, an intergalactic smuggler, or a covert operative. He became a teacher and librarian instead, at least until the CIA calls or aliens abduct him. He's the author of THE RAIDERS OF FOLKLORE series. He's also written DOUBLE CROSS and FATED, two short story prequels to THE EYE OF ODIN, the first book in THE RAIDERS OF FOLKLORE series. He lives in British Columbia, Canada, with his wife and a clowder of black cats.

www.dennisstaginnus.com

CPSIA information can be obtained
at www.ICGtesting.com
Printed in the USA
LVOW13s1741290517
536187LV00010B/487/P